SWEET REVENGE...

Jackman saw Decker heading for the dining room with another woman. He knew he was going to have to move now. Jackman cleared the roulette table, and drew his gun from his shoulder harness.

The heavyset man at the faro table saw the movement and knew what was going to happen.

"Hey, pal!" he shouted.

Decker heard the shout, and pushed Annie Tucker away from him with his left hand. With his right, he dug into his jacket for his gun.

Jackman fired.

Decker felt the bullet hit him in the left shoulder as he pulled his gun free. He dropped down, hoping to avoid being hit a second time, and turned quickly. The man was just starting to fire again when Decker pulled the trigger of his gun. His shot struck the man in the throat, killing him instantly.

ROBERT J. RANDISI

Beauty and the Bounty

LEISURE BOOKS NEW YORK CITY

To Loren D. Estleman

A LEISURE BOOK®

June 2009

Published by

Dorchester Publishing Co., Inc.
200 Madison Avenue
New York, NY 10016

ISBN 10: 0-8439-6127-9
ISBN 13: 978-0-8439-6127-0
E-ISBN: 978-1-4285-0684-8

Visit us on the web at www.dorchesterpub.com.

Beauty and the Bounty

Prologue I

Hannah Brown could only be described as mousey—unless a man was discerning enough to look beyond her obvious physical flaws.

Her flaws included reading eyeglasses and wearing her hair wound tightly on her head in a bun. Her posture left much to be desired and she had difficulty making direct eye contact.

As far as anyone could tell, she was mousey little Hannah Brown.

Except for Willis Holden.

Holden was the manager of the bank where Hannah Brown had worked for the past three weeks, and Willis didn't think she was mousey.

Willis was unhappily married to a shrewish woman who took great pleasure in whining at him day and night. It was no wonder that he was able to look "past" Hannah Brown's faults, seeing only her attributes.

Willis—in his present state of need—saw a

woman who was actually quite pretty, if you took off the glasses and loosened her hair. She had a good figure—her breasts well rounded and firm— which made her especially appealing.

Willis took Hannah under his wing from the very first day she started working in the bank. He was kind to her, even when it was obvious that she was a slow learner. He was patient, even when she made mistakes totaling receipts. He was understanding when she came up short at her window at the end of the day.

Willis Holden was after Hannah Brown, but he didn't think anyone noticed.

Only Hannah Brown did.

Hannah Brown had been playing Willis like a big fish at the end of a hook. She was hauling him in, but not fast enough to frighten him, or lose him.

She constantly went to him with questions, and then was so appreciative—and impressed—when he came right up with the answers.

"Oh, Mr. Holden," she'd say, "you're just so intelligent."

"Oh, Mr. Holden, how do you know so much?"

And then later . . .

"Oh, Willis, I don't know how to thank you!"

As the fourth week of her employment at the Bank of Kenner's Junction, Nevada, they were "Willis" and "Hannah," and she knew he was on the verge of asking her either to dinner, or to work late.

As it turned out, Willis was so anxious that he asked her to work late.

And she agreed.

That evening, after the other employees had left and Willis Holden had locked the door, he beckoned to Hannah and they entered his office.

"You know why you're here, don't you, Hannah?"

She was a little surprised by his boldness, but managed to hide it well.

"I think so, Willis."

Willis smiled at her benevolently. He was a short man with a round belly, but he believed himself to be quite handsome. Hannah, on the other hand, thought he was a comical little man, and was surprised that it had taken her this long to get him alone in the bank.

"I've been watching you since you started working here, Hannah."

"You've been very helpful, Mr. Holden."

"Willis," he said, "I thought we had settled on Willis."

"Yes, of course," she said. "I'm sorry, but I'm a little nervous."

"Nervous?" Willis asked. "There's nothing to be nervous about, Hannah."

He moved behind her chair and put his hands on her shoulders.

"Nothing at all."

Abruptly, she stood up, turned, and threw herself

into his arms. With her lips on his neck she said, "Oh, Willis, I've waited so long for this!"

Willis Holden was thrown off balance both by her boldness, and the force with which she had thrown herself into his arms. He staggered back beneath her weight, but managed to steady himself.

"Hannah . . ." he said, and she pressed her lips to his.

"Willis . . ." she said, and pressed his lips tightly to hers.

"Oh, Willis, not here . . ." she said moments later, pushing herself away from him.

"Why not . . . darling?" he asked breathlessly.

"Oh . . . I just wouldn't feel right."

"We . . . we could go to a hotel."

"Oh no!" she said. "What if your wife should find out. I'd have to leave town and I'd never see you again. I—I couldn't bear that!"

"Then where, darling," he said, groping for her, "where?"

She gave him a sly look and said, "Do you know what excites me?"

"What? What?" he asked, anxiously.

"Oh," she said, looking away, "you'll think I'm wicked."

"I won't, I swear!"

"The vault," she said.

"The vault?"

"Making love," she said, "in the vault, with all that money around us."

"The vault," he said, again. "We could do that."

"Oh, could we?"

"Of course," he said. "I'm the manager of the bank, after all."

"Oh, Willis," she said, throwing her arms around his neck, "let's."

"All right, dear," he said, "come with me."

Willis led her out of his office and to the vault, which he proceeded to open. It was one of those new walk-in vaults, and it had only been in the bank for three months.

He used the combination which he knew by heart and opened it.

"Oh, Willis . . ." Hannah said, with just the right amount of breathless anticipation in her voice. "Do you know what I'd like now?"

"What . . . my sweet?"

"I'd like you to . . . to—I'd like to watch you undress."

"But, of course," he said, and quickly began stripping off his clothes. Clumsily, he tried to take off his pants before removing his shoes, then realized he had to take off the shoes first. He almost fell getting the second one off, and then almost tripped when his pants fell down around his ankles.

Finally he was naked, and Hannah was not impressed.

"Do you know what I'd like to do now, Willis?" she asked, her hands held up in front of her breasts, almost as if she were going to caress herself.

"What?"

"I would like to . . . clean out this vault, and run away with the money."

"Oh, Hannah," he said, "I would love to run away with you—"

"No, not us, Willis," she said, her right hand reaching behind her back as if to undo her dress, "just me."

Suddenly, there was a small gun in her right hand and it was pointed at Willis Holden.

"Hannah . . . sweet—"

"Save it, Willis," she said in a hard-edged, no-nonsense tone. "Move back against that wall and pick up one of those sacks."

"Hannah, darling—"

She cocked the hammer back on the small gun and pointed it at his head.

"Do it, Willis."

Startled and more than a little frightened, he did as he was told.

"Now start filling the sack with money—large bills, only."

"But . . . but most of this money is the payroll for Mr. Kenner's men—"

"Mr. Kenner's men will have to wait a little longer for this month's wages, Willis. Start filling the bag."

Willis obeyed, wondering frantically how he was going to explain this to his depositors—and Mr. Kenner! My God, and his wife!

"Hannah—"

"Keep filling, Willis dear."

He watched the gun in her hand as he filled the sack, and when it was almost too heavy for him to handle he said, "It won't take any more."

"That's quite enough," she said. "Give it to me."

"It's very heavy—" he started to say, but she quickly grabbed the sack from him.

"All right, Willis, now sit down on the floor."

He obeyed, jumping up a bit when his bare butt came into contact with the cold floor.

"Are you going to kill me?" he asked.

"Heavens, no," she said. "I'm just going to leave you in here for a little while."

"You mean, lock me in?"

"That's right."

"But . . . I'll die."

"Nonsense," Hannah said. "There is plenty of air in here for you until someone comes in and lets you out."

"But Hannah—" he babbled, "how can you—I mean, we were—going to—"

"No, Willis," she said, "we weren't going to—not ever!"

With that she slammed the vault door shut so violently that her glasses fell off her nose. She left them on the floor. She opened the sack of money, dropped the gun inside, then grasped it with both hands and lifted it up. She had a buggy waiting outside the back door, and carried the sack to it, depositing it on the front seat. She climbed up onto the buggy and sat next to the sack, pressing her hip against it, enjoying the solid feel of the money inside.

This job had taken her somewhat longer to set up than usual, and she hoped that when she counted the money, it would be worth it.

If it wasn't, she would have to go back to

stagecoaches. There wasn't nearly as much time involved setting up the theft. All she had to do was pose as a passenger, and once they were out in the middle of nowhere, rob it.

She wondered if she should try a train next.

When Hannah Brown reached the horse she had left earlier that day, she stepped down from the buggy and unhitched the other. Next she separated the money from the canvas sack into two saddlebags, which she tossed on her horse's back after saddling him. Next, she set about getting rid of "Hannah Brown."

First, she let her hair down. She longed to wash her auburn hair, because she knew once she did it would take on its true luster. She undressed, discarding "Hannah's" frumpy clothes, and put on a shirt and jeans that did little to hide her lovely figure. She pulled on her boots, making sure that the two-shot derringer she kept in the right one was easily accessible.

When she mounted her horse and readied to leave Nevada for good, "Hannah Brown" was dead, and Julie Landan re-emerged as a wealthy woman.

II

Evanville, Wyoming

Decker finished his breakfast and ordered a second pot of coffee. While he was waiting he took out the two posters and laid them on the table in front of him.

The first poster was for a man named Bill Lutz, who was wanted for bank robbery and assault. The reward was one thousand dollars.

The second poster was more interesting, not only because it was a woman. It was interesting because there were drawings of four different women on it, with four different names—but it was believed that they were all one and the same. This mysterious woman was something of a master of disguise, and used her talents to get into a bank as a teller, or into the employ of a wealthy rancher as a secretary. Sometimes she would run a church raffle and then make off with the money, or con a wealthy woman out of five thousand dollars, with a promise that she could bring the woman's husband back to life.

So this woman was a master of the con, and that interested Decker much more than going after just another bank robber.

He refolded the poster on Bill Lutz and tucked it away for another day.

Over his second pot of coffee he studied the drawings on the woman's poster. Whoever the artist was, he was good. He had worked from witnesses' descriptions and yet, to Decker's practiced eye, there was something similar about all four. The way the eyebrows arched, or the shape of her face. In each case, however, if you did not look as carefully as Decker did, you would swear that the drawings were of four different women.

According to the poster, her last con had been

pulled in a place called Kenner's Junction, Nevada, where she had gotten herself hired as a teller, and then robbed the bank.

Decker finished his coffee, put the woman's poster in a different pocket than the other, and left the cafe.

Outside, he headed for the livery when a young man stepped out into the street, directly in his path.

"Are you Decker?"

"I'm Decker, but I don't know you," Decker said. "What can I do for you?"

"You arrested my brother."

"I don't have the authority to arrest anyone, mister," Decker said.

"Well, you brought him in."

Decker frowned, studying the man.

"Are you Wesley Fairburn?"

"That's right."

"Ah. You're Henry's brother?"

"Yeah."

"Well, Henry had a price on him, Wes, and I brought him in. What's that mean to us, right now?"

"I'm gonna kill you."

"Is that a fact?"

He could see by the look in the man's eyes, and the way his hand shook, that he was scared.

"I'm gonna gun ya, like you gunned my brother."

"I shot your brother in self-defense, friend—and besides, he didn't die."

"That don't matter."

"Sure it does. You see, your brother was wanted alive, and if I had killed him, I wouldn't have collected the bounty."

"So?"

"Well, as far as I know, Wesley, there's no price on your head."

"So?"

"So, that means that there's no sense in me trying to keep you alive. If you go for that gun, I'm going to kill you, pure and simple."

A drop of sweat must have dropped in Wesley Fairburn's eyes, because he flinched and blinked, then wiped his sleeve across his eyes. If Decker had wanted him dead, he could have had him just then, easily.

"You better draw your gun before you blink again, son," Decker said. "If you blink again, you're going to die—that is, unless you walk away right now."

"I . . . I can't," Fairburn said. "I promised my brother."

"You love your brother, huh?"

"S-sure."

"Enough to die for him? For no good reason? I mean, he did what he was wanted for, didn't he?"

Fairburn didn't answer.

"Take my word for it, son, he did it, and he deserves whatever he's going to get. Now I don't know you, but somehow I don't think that you deserve to die just because your brother was stupid. What do you think, Wesley?"

Fairburn looked at Decker and saw a tall, slender, cold-eyed man who was completely at ease. He wasn't even sweating!

"Come on, son, make up your mind. I've got places to go."

Wesley Fairburn stared at Decker a little while longer then suddenly lowered his eyes to the ground. Decker then continued to walk, and as he passed the man he muttered, "Smart decision," and went on by.

He heard Wesley Fairburn move, then, and as his own hand streaked for his gun he went into a crouch. He was not a fast gun, but he knew exactly what he was doing.

Fairburn was so nervous that even when he tried to shoot Decker in the back it didn't work. Decker had crouched, but Fairburn's shot was hurried and off the mark, anyway.

He never got a chance to fire again.

"You're free to go.

Sheriff Sam Tucker handed Decker his gunbelt and stood by while he put it on.

"Guess you got 'em both, Decker."

"Yeah, but I only collected for one," Decker said. "I don't like killing a man for nothing."

"Rather do it for money, huh?"

Decker put the sheriff's remark down to the normal lawman's dislike of bounty hunters. It was not meant as anything personal.

"I don't like killing at all, Sheriff," Decker said.

"You've got Henry in one of your cells, which proves that."

"I guess," Tucker said. He was a big, florid faced man in his fifties who had long since run out of holes on his belt and was making his own.

Decker took out the poster on the woman and handed it to the sheriff.

"What do you know about this woman, Sheriff?"

The lawman looked the poster over and said, "Not much more than is written there. This your next target?"

"Yes."

The lawman handed the poster back.

"How the hell would you start looking for a woman who can change the way she looks?" the sheriff asked. "*Where* would you start looking?"

"She's a con woman, Sheriff," Decker said. "I happen to know the man who invented the word 'con.'"

Chapter One

Duke Ballard had gone by many names during his fifty-one years, but the one his friends always used was Duke.

Duke had been "on the con" since he was ten years old. He had truly refined the art of being someone he was not, and selling someone something that didn't exist.

If the number of trusted friends he had made over the years could be counted on one hand, then the index finger was Decker.

Decker knew where to find Duke these days. He owned a hotel in San Francisco, just a few blocks away from Portsmouth Square, where all the larger hotels and gambling establishments stood.

When Decker rode into the jaded town of San Francisco astride John Henry, his nine-year-old gelding, he commanded attention.

He sat tall and straight in the saddle beneath a flat-brimmed black hat. A well-built man who rode with enough confidence that both women and men looked his way.

If the man alone did not attract attention, there was the hangman's noose, which quickly identified him to one and all, and the weapon he wore on his hip. It was a shotgun that had been sawed off at both the barrels and the stock, and then slipped into a specially made holster. The whole rig had been designed for him by a gunsmith friend when Decker discovered that he was almost hopeless with a handgun. With the shotgun he rarely had to aim to hit what he was shooting at, and with a rifle he was . . . adequate.

After putting John Henry up in the hotel livery, getting in to see Duke wasn't easy, but once Decker convinced the desk clerk that it was in his best interests to announce Decker's presence, he was shown to Duke's suite.

"Decker, goddamn!" Duke said as Decker entered the room. "It *is* you."

The woman behind Duke was still straightening herself out, and beyond both of them Decker could see Duke's rumpled bed.

"Sorry if I interrupted something, Duke."

"Interrupted," Duke said, looking genuinely puzzled. "Oh, you mean . . ." he said, finally catching on. "No, no, I was just . . . interviewing her for a job." He turned around and said, "Why don't you go down to the dining room and have a lunch on me, Laura. I'll talk to you later."

"Sure, Duke."

The woman was tall and blonde, with beautiful blue eyes that held a somewhat vacant look. She had virtually everything a woman should have, except a brain.

After the woman left, Duke rushed Decker and embraced him. It was an odd embrace because Decker was over six feet, while Duke laid claim to being five-foot-five. He had enough power in his arms, however, for a man a foot taller.

"Easy on the ribs!" Decker yelped.

"I'm just so glad to see ya!" Duke said, releasing his friend. "You look fine."

"*You* look fine," Decker said. "You look younger than I do."

"What brings you to San Francisco, Deck? Not hunting a gambling man, are you? They're my meat, you know."

"And potatoes, I know," Decker said. "Speaking of which, how about springing for a meal for an old friend, and I'll tell you the whole story."

"You got it. Let's go downstairs. I've got the best cook in town."

"I'll bet they're glad to hear that over in Portsmouth Square," Decker said.

Once they were seated at a large table at the back of the dining room and Duke had ordered enough food for ten men, Decker told Duke his story.

"Let me see the poster," Duke said, and Decker passed it over. "Are these drawings accurate?"

"Can't tell, but there is sure a similarity between them, don't you think?"

"Sure in the eyes, especially. If she was really

good she'd shave off her eyebrows, and then paint them on to suit her identity for the con."

"She's been real successful up to now, Duke."

"Yeah, but who has she been fooling, Deck?" Duke asked. "Sorry, but I ain't ready to elect her queen of the con women. Not while Lily the Lover and Nowhere Nellie are still plying their trade."

"Nowhere Nellie? I thought she was dead."

"She wanted people to think that for a while, but she's back in circulation, now."

"Jesus, how old is she?"

"Must be sixty, but I swear she's still a good-looking woman—and she can look forty, if she wants to. Now, there's a woman who knows her business. This one," Duke said, tapping the poster, "this one's an amateur."

"Can you find out anything for me about this one?" Decker asked.

Duke touched the poster again.

"I can try. Where was her last job?"

"Nevada."

"Jesus, that means she could even have come here afterward."

"That's possible. That's why I didn't mind coming here to see you."

"Well, if she's in San Francisco I'll find her, that's for sure. If she's not . . . where else has she pulled her jobs?"

"She moves around. New Mexico, Texas, Colorado. If I could find out where she lays low after each job—they're usually a month or two apart."

"Well, there are some places where the people in our fraternity cool off," Duke said. He wasn't talking about him and Decker when he said "our fraternity" but about himself and the other people in the business of running a con. "I could check them, but only because we're friends—and only because she's an amateur. Only an amateur would go after a bank."

Decker knew what Duke Ballard meant. Duke had a lot of friends in the business, and would never help Decker catch any of them. Duke had never gone after a bank—he kept to private people and private concerns.

"Banks, railroads, they've got too much money, and can hire too many people to go looking for you for a long time," Duke had told him a long time ago.

"This could take a few days, you know," Duke said, as the waiter came with the food.

Decker waited until the man had served everything, and then said, "You keep feeding me like this, and it could take a week."

"You eat your fill while you're here. Deck. There's no charge for your room or your meals."

"What about gambling?"

Duke smiled and said, "I got to make my money someway, Decker—and don't let me see you gambling in them fancy Portsmouth Square hotels."

"Duke," Decker said, "your hotel is the last place I'd want to break."

After lunch Duke asked Decker, "You still work the same way?"

"I don't know. What way do you mean?"

"If I know you, you mean to check out the location of her last job. That means you're going to Nevada."

"Already been," Decker said. "Went there before I came here."

"Have any luck?"

"Not much."

"Well, maybe you'll do better here," Duke said, standing up. "I've got some work to do, and I'll get my inquiries started about your lady. Where will you be?"

"Either in the saloon or gambling. You do have a saloon, don't you?"

"Saloon's that way," Duke said, nodding his head in one direction, "and the gambling's that way. I'd appreciate it if you'd take it easy on the first, and overindulge on the second."

"Might do it the other way around."

"Not if I know you," Duke said. "See you later."

As Duke started away he suddenly stopped and then turned.

"Hey Deck? You still carrying that noose around with you?"

"Why wouldn't I be?"

Duke shrugged and said, "No reason," and left the dining room.

After Duke left, Decker decided to finish the coffee that was left in the pot and think about his new quarry. Instead, he found himself thinking about the noose that had almost killed him.

Chapter Two

It happened in Kansas when Decker was about twenty-one. A woman was killed and he was blamed.

He had been hired by the woman's husband to do odd jobs around their ranch and she showed more than a passing interest in him. She was older than Decker by about ten years, and married, and although it wasn't easy, Decker managed to decline her advances. Although she was very beautiful, her husband had hired him to work, and that was what he wanted to do.

Unfortunately, she did not take his rejection kindly, and told her husband he tried to rape her, so he fired Decker.

That was an oversimplification, really. What actually happened was that Decker and the man had a big fight, during which Decker knocked the man down in front of his wife. Doubly embarrassed, the man fired Decker and never paid him the money he owed him for the work he'd already done. That was fine with Decker, though. He just wanted to get away from the two of them.

He was leaving town on foot when the posse rode up on him and arrested him for raping and killing her.

The husband had told them that Decker did it and the case got all the way to court. The judge, eager to make a name for himself with a sensational case, convicted him on flimsy evidence.

The sheriff of the town, a man named Mike Farrell, had believed in Decker's innocence, but Decker was convicted and sentenced to hang.

Even now Decker could feel the noose around his neck.

He actually got as far as the gallows, with the hangman putting the noose over his neck before Mike Farrell brought the real killer in and made him confess.

It was the husband.

Apparently Decker wasn't the first one that the woman had thrown herself at, and that, combined with the fact that Decker knocked the husband down in front of his wife, made the man angry enough to attack his own wife, raping her and then killing her.

Nobody apologized. By the time Decker stepped down from the gallows, everyone had left. They'd gone home disappointed that they weren't going to see a hanging.

The sheriff resigned and left town after that. Decker rode with him for a short time. Farrell tried to get Decker to take up being a lawman, but he had other ideas.

He became a bounty hunter. His reasoning was that he wanted to get to the ones who were going to be hanged and satisfy himself that they were guilty before he handed them over to the law. He didn't want what happened to him to happen to any other innocent man—ever.

The noose that he carried was a reminder of what almost happened to him, and of why he took up bounty hunting. He lost sight of his reasons once in a while, but the noose always brought it back to him.

Decker shook his head, dispelling the thoughts of the past, and thought instead of his very recent trip to Kenner's Junction, the scene of the last bank robbery.

Chapter Three

When Decker rode into Kenner's Junction, Nevada, he wasn't impressed. He wondered how the woman on the poster had known that there would be a substantial sum of money in the bank safe. She must have known that even before she took a job there, or else why pose as a teller?

He put his horse up at the livery and since it was late afternoon went to the hotel to book a room. It would take some time for him to ask his questions, and by then it would be getting dark. Better to spend the night.

He got his room, unloaded his gear, and went looking for the saloon. Bartenders were usually the first ones he spoke to in a new town. They knew more than most people, and usually knew more than they would tell.

"What can I get ya?" this bartender asked. He was a tall, skinny man in his forties with a big nose and jutting jaw. The fact that his neck could only be described as scrawny made the picture all the more odd.

"Whiskey."

"Bottle?"

"Did I ask for a bottle?"

"Nope. I just figured you for the thirsty type."

The bartender set down a shot glass of whiskey and said, "Two bits."

Decker dropped the coin on the bar and asked, "Who's the law hereabouts?"

"That'd be Ed Friendly."

"Are you kidding?"

The bartender laughed and said, "That's his name, friend."

"Been here long?"

"Me or the sheriff?"

"The sheriff."

" 'bout two years. Up for reelection soon, and I reckon he'll make it."

"This bank robbery I heard about. That won't hurt him in the election?"

"Naw. Only people that hurt was Mr. Kenner and Willis Holden."

"Who's Holden?"

"Bank manager."

"He get blamed for the robbery?"

"Who gets blamed for a robbery?" the barkeep asked. "It happens. Caught hell from his wife, though."

"What for?"

"Hell, he was found naked as a jaybird in the vault, and that mousey little teller turned up missing."

"Mousey?"

"Well, some might have thought she was attractive, but she kind of just blended in with the walls, if you know what I mean. Most men prefer their women a little more . . . noticeable."

Unless she was deliberately trying to go unnoticed.

"And what about Kenner?"

"Kenner, as in Kenner's Junction. He's got a big spread nearby, and it was his payroll got stolen. He had to front another one for his men."

"Sounds decent enough."

"Oh, he's a decent man, all right. He didn't fire Holden."

"Kenner owns the bank?"

"Sure, and several other businesses in town."

"I see." Decker set his empty glass down.

"Another?"

"No, thanks. I suppose if Willis Holden didn't get fired I'd find him at the bank?"

"Sure enough."

"Which way?"

"Out the door, make a right and two blocks."

"And the sheriff's office?"

"A block beyond that."

"Much obliged."

"Sure."

When Decker left the saloon he decided to make his stops in order. First he'd stop by the bank and talk to Willis Holden, and then by the sheriff's office to talk to the lawman with the unlikely name of Ed Friendly.

Chapter Four

Decker found Willis Holden a singularly unimpressive individual. He was slight, weak-chinned and quite possibly weak-willed. He looked like the perfect picture of a henpecked husband. How, Decker wondered, had he managed to end up naked in the vault?

Decker got in to see Holden by mentioning the bank robbery. Holden came rushing out, as if he thought Decker might have brought the money back.

"Mr. Decker?"

"Yes."

"So nice to meet you, sir," Holden said, pumping Decker's hand. "You said you had some information about the bank robbery that took place a couple of weeks ago?"

"Would it be possible for us to talk in your office, Mr. Holden?"

"Hmm? Oh, of course. Follow me."

Willis Holden led Decker into an office that was equally as unimpressive as the man himself.

Decker guessed that Holden had probably furnished it himself, apparently as inexpensively as possible.

"Now, this information that you have—" Holden began, but Decker cut him off.

"I didn't say I had information on the robbery, Mr. Holden."

"I'm sorry, but I thought—"

"I just want to ask you some questions about it, Mr. Holden."

"Questions?" Holden asked. Decker noticed that his voice rose a bit, and almost squeaked nervously. "What sort of questions?"

"How it happened, really. You see, I'm hunting the woman who held you up."

"Hunting?"

"Yes, I'm a bounty hunter, and anything I can learn about her would aid me in finding her."

"And getting my money back?"

Not bloody likely, Decker thought wryly.

"Possibly."

"Well . . . I'll help in any way I can."

"I would need the truth, Mr. Holden."

"Of course."

"And it would go no further than this room."

"Hmm?" Holden did not look completely convinced, but finally agreed. "Well, what questions do you have?"

Decker leaned forward and said, "Just how did it come about that you were . . . naked?"

"Well . . ." Holden blustered, "she had a gun—"

"But what happened before that?"

"I . . . don't know what you mean."

"I mean, did she use her . . . charms on you?"

"Mr. Decker, anyone will tell you that Miss Brown . . . or whatever her name really was, was quite plain looking."

"Perhaps that's what she wanted people to think? I have a poster on her, and along with your description, it has three other drawings of her." Decker handed Holden the poster and said, "As you can see, in the other three drawings she's quite attractive."

"Hmm," Holden said, studying the drawings intensely.

"Perhaps you were able to see past her disguise? I mean, a man as observant as yourself . . ."

"Well," Holden said, handing the poster back, "perhaps I did see through her . . . somewhat."

"And found her attractive?"

Holden attempted to loosen his collar and said, "Uh, yes, somewhat."

"Believe me, Mr. Holden, our discussion will go no further than this room."

"Perhaps I was a bit . . . taken with her, which made it easier for her to . . . get me into a compromising position and then . . . take advantage of it."

"I see. She didn't produce the gun until . . ."

"Until we were in the vault."

"Ah. And by that time you were . . . already . . . undressed?"

"Ahem . . . yes."

"Did she make any friends while she was here? Fellow workers?"

"I don't . . . well, I did see her talking to Amy Butterworth on occasion."

"Amy?"

"She's a teller in the bank."

"Is she . . . attractive?"

"Quite."

How did Decker miss her when he came in.

"I believe she's out to lunch now, but she should be back shortly."

"Perhaps I'll stop by later, after I've seen the sheriff," Decker said, standing up.

"The sheriff?" Holden said. "You won't . . ."

"No, Mr. Holden, I won't tell the sheriff anything that we've discussed here."

"Thank you, Mr. Decker. You see—well, my wife . . . ah, you understand."

"Yes, Mr. Holden," Decker said, heading for the door, "I understand perfectly."

Chapter Five

Ed Friendly was far from friendly looking, and the condition extended to his attitude—especially toward bounty hunters.

"Don't like you fellas," Friendly said when Decker introduced himself, "never did, never will."

"I don't have a problem with that, Sheriff," Decker said. "I can understand it."

"You can?"

"Sure. You do your job for a monthly wage—a low wage—and you see people like me walking away with the big rewards."

"Yeah, that's right."

"But that wouldn't make you help an outlaw get away, would it?"

"What outlaw are we talking about?"

"The woman who robbed your bank."

"Her! She made a fool of Holden, that one did. And he thinks his wife doesn't know what he was up to."

"She does?"

"Of course she does. She's a fine woman, Rachel Holden is. A fine woman."

"I wonder how she found out?"

"She's not a stupid woman."

"Obviously not. Anyway, is there anything that you can tell me about the robber?"

"Not much. She didn't talk to a lot of people. You know, kept to herself."

"How long was she here?"

"A couple of months."

"And she didn't make any friends in all that time?"

"Didn't you ask Holden that?"

"He mentioned Amy, a teller in the bank, but what about male friends?

The lawman smirked and said, "You should probably have asked Holden about that, too."

Yes, Decker thought, I should have. He didn't relish talking to Holden again, however, and decided instead to talk to Amy Butterworth about it.

"All right, Sheriff," Decker said, "thanks for your help."

"Wasn't much help, if you ask me."

"Well, that shouldn't distress you much, Friendly, seeing how you feel about bounty hunters."

"You're right about that. How long will you be staying in town, Decker?"

"Just overnight," Decker assured him. "I'll be leaving in the morning."

"Good," Friendly said, "that's good."

"Have a nice day," Decker said.

After Decker left, the lawman folded his hands under his chin and stared at the door. Damned bounty hunters, got all the reward money.

He wondered how good he would be at it.

When Decker arrived back at the bank he found Amy Butterworth in her teller's cage. He managed to convince her to give him a few moments of her time.

She was almost pretty, blonde, with very fair eyebrows and lashes and a slender form.

"I guess I'm the only one she ever really talked to," Amy said, "but then, I suppose it was all lies."

"Maybe it wasn't," Decker said. "Amy, would you be willing to let me buy you dinner?"

"But . . . you're a stranger," the girl said.

"I assure you, my only intention is to talk about Hannah Brown."

"Hmph," Amy said then. "I'll bet that wasn't even her real name."

"What about dinner?" he asked the hopelessly naive girl.

Over dinner Amy did two things very well—she ate and she talked. Decker was hard put to decide which she did faster.

He listened very intently as she relayed some of the things "Hannah Brown" had told her, and he filed them away for future reference.

Now, sitting in Duke Ballard's hotel in San Francisco, he thought about some of those things.

She'd talked about being hurt by a man. Decker had a hunch that was true.

She spoke of having something to prove in a world controlled by men. Decker felt that was true, also. That was why she was doing what no self respecting con *man* would do, using her abilities on banks, and other institutions.

This woman lived to compete with men. Decker wondered how he'd be able to use that against her.

He was preparing to go to bed when there was a knock at his door. When he opened it, he was surprised to find a woman standing there. She was tall and slender, wearing a low-cut gown that showed off her creamy white firm breasts. Her hair was blonde, and worn in a single long pony tail that hung over her right shoulder.

"Hello," she said, smiling.

"Uh, hello."

"Can I come in?"

"I, uh, do you have the right room?" he asked, puzzled.

"Are you Decker?" she asked. "Duke's friend?"

"Uh, yes, I am, but—"

"Then I have the right room," she said, moving past him into the room . . .

Chapter Six

The next morning while Decker was waiting for his breakfast, Duke joined him.

"Clean me out last night?" Duke asked.

"I broke even."

"Bad sign," Duke said. "You'll either lose big or win big today."

"Is that your experience?"

"It certainly is. By the way, did you have a pleasant night?" Duke asked this question with a hopelessly smug look on his face.

"Once I got over the shock, yes, it was very pleasant."

"I'm glad to hear it."

"Do me a favor, though, will you?"

"What?"

"Let me arrange for my own companionship from now on?"

"If that's the way you want it."

"I do."

The waiter came over and took Duke's order, who

simply told him to bring whatever Decker had ordered.

"I've got something for you on your con lady," Duke said after the waiter had left.

"Already?"

"My community is a pretty small one," Duke said, "and your girlfriend is making waves."

"What kind of waves?"

"Like I said yesterday, she's doing things only an amateur would do—but she's getting away with it. It's not making her very popular."

"Because she's getting away with it?"

"Because she's breaking the rules."

"Oh," Decker said, "the rules . . ."

"The rules of the game, Decker."

"Well, Duke, maybe to her it's not a game."

"It's all a game, Decker. If she doesn't know that, she's dangerous."

"Tell me something, Duke. Is she impressing anyone?"

"She is."

"You?"

Duke shook his head.

"No, not me."

"So what's being said?"

"The feeling is that she's been building up to something."

"What?"

"Look at her pattern. Texas, New Mexico, Arizona, Nevada—"

"California," Decker guessed. "And I'd lay odds

she'd come to San Francisco."

"That's the general feeling. If she can come here and pull off a big con, then she'd really impress people."

"So all I have to do is wait for her."

"It might take a while, but no longer than if you went out looking for her. Make yourself comfortable here. Gamble, sightsee, chase some women—and wait."

"I don't know—"

"If you ask me, you look as if you could use the rest. Why don't you just forget about her for a while? Take some time off, for Chrissake! Or do you need the money that badly?"

"Not the money, not that badly," Decker said. "Not yet, anyway."

"Then what is it? The action? Is that what you need? Believe me, Decker, there's plenty of action here in San Francisco."

"I'm sure there is."

"Good, then it's settled. You'll stay here—on the house, of course."

"Hey, Duke, that's fine for a few days, but—"

"As long as you like, Decker," Duke scolded him, "you know that."

Decker smiled as breakfast arrived and said, "How can I turn down an offer like that?"

"You can't."

That settled, they both turned their attention to breakfast. Decker didn't know if he could completely push "Hannah Brown" from his mind while he was in San Francisco, but he could damn well try.

* * *

For the next three days Decker gambled, looked at San Francisco, ate well, even spent some time in the company of several lovely women.

By the fourth day, the inactivity had worn thin.

"I'm going crazy," he told Duke on the morning of the fourth day, over breakfast.

"Well, actually," Duke told him, "you've lasted a lot longer than I thought you would."

"Smart guy."

"I've got something that might interest you."

"Information on my con lady?"

"No," Duke said, "a special poker game, starting tonight."

"Where?"

"In one of the suites."

"What do you mean by a special game?"

"You need an invitation to play, and you need to be a damned good player."

"Who's playing?"

"Some friends of mine."

"Friends of yours," Decker said, looking dubious. "I could go broke playing poker with friends of yours."

"They're all gamblers," Duke assured him, "not a con man—or woman—among them."

"Name one."

"Luke Short."

Decker's eyebrows shot up.

"I've never met Short."

"That makes you even. He's never met you, either."

"Are you inviting me to observe this game—or play in it?"

"What good would you do just observing? Of course you'll play."

"When?"

"Tonight. We'll have dinner together, and then I'll take you up."

"All right," Decker agreed, but he was doubtful that even the most interesting poker game would be able to keep his attention and interest indefinitely. Eventually, he was going to have to get back to the only thing that really kept his interest.

The hunt.

Chapter Seven

When Duke showed up for dinner that night Decker was surprised to see that he was with a woman. She was a stunning redhead who put the blonde from the night before to shame.

Decker stood up as Duke and the woman approached the table.

"Decker, meet Stella Morrell. Stella, this is my friend Decker."

"I'm pleased to meet you, Mr. Decker."

"Just Decker," Decker said.

"I've heard so much about you from Duke."

"Shall we sit down?" Duke said.

"Please," Decker said. Duke held Stella Morrell's chair for her, and then sat down across from Decker.

"I thought we had a deal," Decker said to Duke. He was referring to their agreement that Decker would arrange for his own companionship.

"Stella is here for the poker game, Decker," Duke explained. "She's the only woman invited."

"You must find that quite an honor," Decker said.

He felt embarrassed at having mistaken her for a whore.

"Oh, I don't know. Is it an honor to sit in a smoke-filled room full of men, all of whom will be undressing me with their eyes."

"While you take their money," Decker said.

She smiled and said, "Yes, there is that."

He saw that she was not young, probably in her mid-thirties, but he was willing to bet that she was more beautiful now than she had ever been before. She struck him as one of those women who would grow even more lovely as she got older.

"Will you be playing also, Mr. Decker?"

"I've invited him," Duke said.

"Well, if you've been invited, then you must play. I can assure you, it will be a very interesting game."

"How long will the game go on?" Decker asked.

Duke laughed and Stella said, "Until somebody wins."

Obviously, it was the kind of game that could go on for days. Decker liked playing poker, and could sit and play for hours, but days? The only thing that he could do for days—and weeks, and sometimes months—was hunt.

Decker had become a bounty hunter out of necessity, but he soon discovered that it was all he was really cut out to do. He spent many weeks out on the trail alone, tracking his prey, and never gave it a second thought. There were a lot of people in San Francisco, and soon he knew that the city would start to close in on him.

He couldn't even think of staying in one room with five or six other people for days, with only short breaks for sleep and food.

"Tell me something," he said, "can someone play in this game only for a few hours?"

"You can play as long as you like," Duke said, "but the game will be going on for a long time, with players sitting in and dropping out."

"It will be very interesting," Stella said.

"I'm sure it will be," Decker said.

They ordered dinner, and conversation was kept very light. No deep, dark secrets or life's goals were discussed at the table, and when dinner was done Duke said, "Well, shall we go up?"

"By all means," Stella said. She turned her green eyes on Decker and asked, "Will you be coming, Mr. Decker."

"For a while, anyway," Decker said. "For a little while."

There was a huge round table in the center of the suite, and off to one side a small sidebar, where five men were standing, some drinking, some smoking, some doing both.

When Duke made the introductions, Decker was impressed. He recognized three of the five names, including that of Luke Short.

Short was smaller than Decker thought he would be. He was a dapper man with a mustache, a firm grip and a steady eye.

The others he recognized were Gentleman Dan Patrick, and Eddie Black.

The remaining two men in the room were introduced as Jordan Shaker and Sam Gibson.

"Can we get this game under way now?" Gibson asked. He was a big man in his mid-forties who wore an ill fitting black suit—ill fitting because his belly was so large.

"By all means," Duke said.

As they sat down Decker discovered that Duke was not going to play. He would simply deal, and when he was not dealing a relief dealer would be brought in.

With Duke dealing and not playing, there were seven players. After they had all changed cash into chips, they were ready to start.

"I thought Dutch Leonard was going to be here," Luke Short commented.

"Dutch might be arriving tomorrow," Duke said. "I know he was intending to come. We'll just have to wait and see."

"And Tim Champlin?"

"Tim can't make it this time."

"What about Clark Howard?" Dan Patrick said. "I played in a game with him two months back, and he said he was going to come."

"He'll definitely be arriving tomorrow," Duke said. "This is the first hand of the night, gentlemen and lady. Five card stud."

Duke dealt out the cards, and Decker caught a King. Eddie Black had an Ace, and he opened for twenty dollars.

The game was starting out small.

* * *

Decker was out of his class.

He knew that almost from the beginning, but a streak of luck kept him in the game for the first three hours. Halfway through the fourth hour he had lost half of what he'd won during the first three hours. Decker's back was beginning to hurt and he decided to call it a night.

"If you gentlemen—and the lady—don't mind, I think I'll hang it up for now."

"Your choice," Duke said. "Anybody can quit at any time."

Decker picked up what was left of his winnings and cashed in his chips with Duke.

"I could use a drink and a short rest," Stella Morrell said. "Would you mind?"

"No, not at all," Decker said.

Stella did not cash in, indicating that she was returning very soon.

Chapter Eight

They left the room together and went down to the empty hotel dining room, where they took a table and ordered drinks.

"You were lucky," Stella said, "in the beginning of the game."

"You noticed."

"Yes, I did."

"I'm sure everyone did," Decker said. "I'm hopelessly out of my depth up there. The cards just happened to be coming right for the first few hours. Anybody could have won with them."

"I wouldn't necessarily say you were out of your depth—not hopelessly, anyway." He thought she was just being generous. "Everyone up there does this for a living, Decker. You did quite well for someone who only plays for fun."

"Relaxation," he said, "only right now I feel anything but relaxed."

"Yes," she said, looking amused, "I noticed that your back is a little stiff."

"Is it that obvious?"

"You kept stretching on the way down."

"I still am," he said, and demonstrated. "I'm used to sitting in the saddle for hours at a time, but those hard wood chairs . . ."

They made some more small talk; Stella gave him some pointers on improving his game. When their drinks were almost gone Decker said, "You didn't invite yourself down here to talk about poker."

She paused, then said, "No, I didn't. Duke tells me you . . . hunt people for a living."

"I'm a bounty hunter," he said. "Let's not make it sound like anything else."

"All right, fine. You're a bounty hunter. Would I be able to hire you to find someone?"

"No."

She frowned.

"Why not?"

"Because I don't hire out."

"You do find people for money, don't you?"

"I hunt people for the bounty on them," Decker said. "There's a difference. What you need is a private detective agency, like Pinkerton."

"No."

"I wish I could help you, Stella—"

"Do you only hunt people that you can kill to bring the bodies back, then? Is it because I want my . . . this person brought back alive?"

"You're upset," Decker said, "and you're saying things you don't mean."

"Yes, you are probably right," she said. "This is very important to me, Decker. I would pay you a lot of money to take this . . . this job."

"I'm sorry, Stella," Decker said, with genuine regret. "I wish I could help you.

"Yes," she said, coldly, "so do I." She stood up, threw some money down on the table for her drink and said, "I'm sorry I took up your valuable time."

"Stella—" he said, but she stormed away without looking back. On the way out she passed Duke, who paused to say something to her, but was ignored.

As Duke approached Decker's table Decker said, "I thought you were dealing."

"I brought in the relief man when I saw you and Stella leave together. What did you do to her?"

"Nothing."

"Something's got her all riled up."

"Did you know that she was going to ask me to find someone for her?"

"Someone? Who?"

"I don't know who," Decker said. "Don't you?"

Duke sat down and said, "You mean, like a missing person?"

"I suppose so."

Duke shrugged and said, "Why would I have any idea, Decker?"

"She said you were the one who told her I find people."

"I told her what you do for a living, sure. That's no secret. If she took it the wrong way, that's her problem. Does she want you to find somebody with a price on his head?"

"I don't know. All I know is she asked if she could hire me to find someone."

"And you said no?"

"Of course. I don't hire out, Duke. You know that."

"Sure, I know that."

"I hope I haven't put you in bad with her by refusing."

"Not me, but do you know that you probably could have had that lady in your bed tonight, if you had said yes?"

"Fortunately, my morals and yours have never been introduced."

"All right," Duke said, shrugging helplessly, "if you don't *want* a woman who looks like that in your bed."

"I certainly wouldn't kick her out of bed," Decker said, "providing she came there of her own free will in the first place."

Looking injured Duke said, "I have never taken a woman to my bed who wasn't willing to go."

"Your kind of 'willing' and mine are just not the same thing."

"If we're so different, how come we're friends?" Duke asked.

"I always need a father figure," Decker said, standing up.

"Ouch!"

"I'm turning in."

"How about having a drink with me?"

"I'm too tired."

"Who's the father figure now?" Duke asked.

"In the morning I'd like you to give me some idea where I might start looking for my con lady here in San Francisco."

Duke made a face.

"Are you getting on that again?"

"It's what I do, Duke," Decker said. "It's what I should have been doing all along instead of playing these games. Well, game time is over, and it's time to get back to work."

"If that's the way you want it."

"It's not the way I want it, Duke," Decker said, "it's just the way it is."

Chapter Nine

"What have you got for me?" Decker asked Duke at breakfast.

Actually, he asked him that question *after* breakfast. *During* breakfast they talked about the poker game.

Duke looked very tired this morning and Decker figured that he had gone back to the game after he'd left him the night before.

"What time did you deal 'til?"

"I don't remember. Four? Five?"

"Did Stella go back to the game?"

"No, and I thought that was odd. It's not like her to quit while she's behind."

"Is she doing badly?"

"Not too badly."

"Who's the big winner?"

"Eddie Black. He's such a straightforward card player that even when he does bluff, nobody believes he's bluffing. Every so often he springs a big one."

"Who's the best player?"

Duke grinned and said, "We could debate that one all day, but my guess is Luke Short—and when Clark Howard shows up, he's almost as good."

Once breakfast was out of the way and they had a second pot of coffee on the table, Decker asked his question.

"Still determined?" Duke asked. When Decker didn't answer Duke sighed.

"Okay, it's pretty cut and dried where she'd be if she's here in San Francisco."

"Where?"

"The big hotels. If she's got money, she's going to want to enjoy it."

"And if she's not here?"

"If she's not here, she could have gone the other way."

"What do you mean?"

"Back east. New York, maybe."

"You think that's likely?"

"No. There's more gambling here."

Decker started to think that maybe he'd made a mistake coming here. He was more comfortable following a trail on horseback, no matter how faint it was. Here in San Francisco there were just too many damned people, and too many places to hide.

Still, he'd started this, and he was determined to finish it.

"So then I simply start making the rounds of all the hotels in Portsmouth Square?"

"Not only the Square."

"She wouldn't go down to the Barbary Coast, or Chinatown, would she?"

"Let's examine what we know about this woman, Deck. She's unorthodox, to say the least. She takes on big odds when she works a bank, or a stage. Would a lady like that be afraid of a Barbary Coast saloon, or a Chinatown gambling den?"

"No, she'd welcome the challenge."

"That's right. My guess is if she's here she'll dress up to the nines and try everything. You're looking at one very attractive lady who more than likely is gonna be somewhere where she sticks out like a sore thumb   and you might find her in the Square, with all the other dressed up swells."

"That's great," Decker said. "What you're telling, me is that she could be anywhere in San Francisco."

"That's what I'm telling you."

"I didn't need you to tell me that, Duke."

Duke smiled and spread his hands.

"You're my friend, Deck. I want to see you relax and have a good time."

"So you keep me waiting for information I could have figured out myself."

"Waiting and relaxing."

"Well, the relaxing is over," Decker said, "and so is the waiting."

Decker stood up to leave, and Duke said, "Wait for me."

"What for?"

Duke stood up and said, "You can't go into the Square looking like that. I'm taking you to my tailor to get you a decent suit."

"What the hell do I need a—"

"If you don't get a decent suit, Decker," Duke said, "you're the one who's going to stick out like a sore thumb."

Chapter Ten

Decker was real uncomfortable.

The black broadcloth suit he was wearing cost more than what he'd probably spent on clothes in the past year, and yet he had to admit that Duke had been right. If he'd walked into a Portsmouth Square hotel wearing anything less expensive, he would have been the center of attention.

Besides, Duke had paid for it and told Decker he could take his time paying him back.

Then there was the gun he was wearing in a shoulder rig. A short-barreled .45. It was Duke's and he'd loaned it to Decker so he wouldn't walk into one of those hotels wearing a gun on his hip. That was another way of attracting attention.

So dressed the way he was, Decker should have gone unnoticed when he walked into the Alhambra—but he didn't.

A man playing the roulette wheel happened to look up as Decker entered, and froze. He didn't even notice when his number came up, and for that reason left the money to ride again, and lost it on the next spin.

Decker didn't notice the man, and probably wouldn't have recognized him even if he had.

Decker walked through the casino, examining the women. Some of them examined him back, others turned their heads away, still others did not notice. As far as Decker was concerned, none of these women fit the bill. He had a hunch that he'd know the right woman when he saw her.

"Are you alone?"

He turned in the direction of the voice and saw a pretty young woman with dark hair and a low bodice.

"Yes."

"Looking for some company?"

"What kind of company?"

"Somebody to help you lose your money."

He laughed. She probably worked for the hotel as a shill, but he liked her.

"Where would you suggest we lose it first?"

"How about blackjack?"

"Let's go."

She linked her arm in his and led him over to the blackjack table.

On the first deal he got blackjack, and had to be paid off immediately. On the second deal it took three cards, but once again he was dealt twenty-one, and was paid off.

"You're gonna make me lose my job if you keep that up," she said, pulling him away from the table.

Suddenly, she realized what she had said and put her hand to her mouth. "I didn't mean—"

"Don't worry," he said. "I figured you worked for the hotel."

"We're not supposed to tell—"

"How about a drink?" he asked. "I can't win any money buying you a drink."

"All right."

She walked him through a large, ornately decorated dining room to a long, mahogany bar.

"What will you have?" he asked.

"Champagne," she said, automatically. "I'm sorry, I'm supposed to—"

"Get the lady some champagne," he said, "and I'll have a beer." He looked at her and said, "It's all right, don't worry about it."

She smiled wanly.

"Are you new at this?"

She nodded and said, "Brand new."

"First night?"

She nodded.

He leaned over and asked, "First customer?"

She hesitated, and then nodded.

The drinks came and he handed her the glass of champagne, and picked up his beer.

"Here's to your first night on the job."

She smiled and sipped her champagne, then wrinkled her nose.

"I've never tasted champagne before."

"What's your name?"

"Sally Tucker. What's yours?"

"Decker. How did you get this job, Sally?"

"My sister works here. She talked to the boss. I think she's sleeping with him."

"And what about you?"

"What do you mean?"

"Are you prepared to sleep with your customers if you have to?"

"Mr. Van Gelder didn't say anything about that."

"Van Gelder. He owns this place?"

"Yes."

"What did he say was your job?"

"To get the men to spend money, or lose it."

"But not to sleep with them?"

"No . . . I don't think so."

"You'd better ask your sister about that."

"Why . . . do you want to sleep with me?"

He gave her a frank appraisal. Beneath the makeup she was wearing she appeared to be all of nineteen, but she filled the dress out firmly, with enough creamy cleavage to attract any man.

"I'd have to be crazy not to want to . . . but that wasn't what I had in mind when I came in."

"Aren't I . . . attractive enough?" she asked. Just a couple of sips of champagne seemed already to be having an effect on her.

"You're lovely, Sally. I just have some other business to attend to."

"I see."

He couldn't figure out if she was afraid he'd say yes, or insulted that he'd said no.

"Sally . . . uh, you're not a virgin, are you?"

"Of course not," she said, her face reddening.

"Well, not exactly, anyway. I mean, I've been with a man . . . twice."

"I see."

"It was back home, in Kansas. Andy Tyler lived nearby, and was always after us—"

"Us?"

"Me and my sisters. The Tyler boys—there was four of them. Andy was the oldest, and they were always sniffing around us. Pa told us to stay away from them, but Annie—she's my sister who works here—she took all four of them into the barn every once in a while, even the younger one, Johnny—he was only fourteen years old."

"Your sister sounds like a lot of fun."

"Anyway, after Annie left and came to San Francisco, the Tyler boys expected me and my other sister—Denise, she's younger than me by a couple of years—they expected us to take up where Annie left off."

"And you did?"

"Only to keep them away from Denise," she said, defensively. "I did it with Andy twice, and then Pa found out and ran them off." She started to laugh and then said, "He filled little Johnny's butt full of birdshot."

He noticed that she was almost finished with her glass of champagne, and was already tipsy. Champagne was certainly new to her.

"Where's your sister now?"

"She's in the casino. She said she found a live one, a big heavyset man with a red face and a full wallet."

"Why don't you wait here. I want to meet her."

"You won't have trouble finding her, she looks like me—only prettier. I'll wait here and have another little glass of champagne."

He left her there and went to find her sister. It was none of his business, but he didn't think Sally belonged in a place like the Alhambra.

Chapter Eleven

Lou Jackman saw Decker come out of the dining room and breathed a sigh of relief. He had thought he'd lost sight of the bounty hunter who'd killed his father. It had happened four years ago, but Jackman remembered it as if it were yesterday. He'd sworn on his father's grave that he'd find Decker and kill him, but he had never run across his trail—until now.

He pushed away from the roulette table and kept his eyes on Decker.

Decker knew Annie Tucker as soon as he saw her standing at the faro table. She was several years older than her sister, Sally, and very beautiful. The resemblance was strong between the two women—the black hair, the creamy cleavage.

"Excuse me," he said, approaching her. "Miss Tucker?"

Annie Tucker turned away from the heavyset man whose arm she was holding and looked at Decker. "Do I know you?" she asked.

"No, ma'am, but I know your sister."

"Sally?"

"Yes, ma'am."

"What about her?"

"She's in the bar, drunk."

"You got her drunk?"

"One glass of champagne got her drunk, and if she were with another man, Miss Tucker, she'd probably already be in a hotel room, undressed."

"Oh?" Annie Tucker said, raising one eyebrow. "But not with you?"

"No, ma'am, not with me. It's probably none of my business, Miss Tucker, but I don't think Sally belongs here."

"Hey, friend," the heavyset man said, looking past Annie Tucker at Decker, "go get your own girl. This one's bringing me luck."

"Take it easy, pal. I'm just talking to her."

The man turned and pushed Annie Tucker away so that he could face Decker. He was not as tall as Decker, but he outweighed him by fifty pounds easily—and not all of it was fat.

"I know you're talking to her. I told you to go find somebody else."

There was a tense moment when Decker thought things were going to get out of hand, but Annie Tucker's quick thinking solved the problem. She rose onto her toes and spoke into the man's ear.

"Oh, yeah?" he said.

"Yes," she said. "I'll only be a moment."

"Well, all right." The man looked at Decker and

said, "The little lady just saved you from a beating, friend."

"I'll have to thank her for it."

"You do that."

"Come on," Annie Tucker said taking Decker's arm. "Show me where she is."

Jackman saw Decker heading for the dining room with another woman. He knew he was going to have to move now. Jackman cleared the roulette table, and drew his gun from his shoulder harness.

The heavyset man at the faro table saw the movement and knew what was going to happen.

"Hey, pal!" he shouted.

Decker heard the shout, and pushed Annie Tucker away from him with his left hand. With his right he dug into his jacket for his gun, but snagged the gun on his jacket.

Decker felt the bullet hit him in the left shoulder as he pulled his gun free. He dropped down, hoping to avoid being hit a second time, and turned quickly. The man was just starting to fire again when Decker pulled the trigger of his gun. His shot struck the man in the throat, killing him instantly.

Then his shoulder started to hurt . . . real bad!

Chapter Twelve

Two of the Alhambra dealers took Decker into a huge office, which Decker assumed belong to the owner, Van Gelder. Moments later, a bearded man came storming in and began shouting loudly.

"What the hell is going on here?"

The two men who had helped Decker into the office stood at attention, as if they were in the army and this man was their superior officer. Annie Tucker had instructed them to move Decker to the office until a doctor and the law could arrive.

"I'm going to take care of Sally," she had told Decker, "and then I'll be right back."

"Fine."

Now Van Gelder glared at both of his men, waiting for an answer.

"I can answer that," Decker said.

"Who are you?"

"Decker. Who are you?"

"Van Gelder, I own this establishment. I hope you're not bleeding on the leather of that sofa."

"I'm doing my best not to."

Someone had given Decker a tablecloth, which he had wadded up and pushed between his jacket and shirt, to try and stem the bleeding.

There was a small crowd outside the office. Van Gelder had to push through it, as a man shouted, "Let me through, please let me through."

A small, elderly man carrying a black medical bag finally entered the office, looked around and then said to Decker, "I guess you're my patient."

"I guess so."

"Let's have a look, then."

Van Gelder looked at his two dealers and said, "All right, you two, get back out there. There are still people in the place looking to lose their money."

The both nodded, and as they headed for the door Decker called out, "Thanks for the help, fellas."

They waved and kept going.

"You were going to tell me what happened," Van Gelder said to Decker.

"One of your patrons shot me in the back."

"Just like that?"

"Just like that."

"And what did you do?"

"I killed him."

"Just—"

"Just like that."

"Who was it?"

"I haven't the faintest idea."

"Stop talking and turn around," the doctor said. "I have to have a look."

Decker stopped talking and turned so that the doctor could get at his wound.

"We'll have to take this jacket off."

"Please, watch the leather," Van Gelder said.

Outside the crowd was once again moving aside to admit someone. When the man entered, he had another man in tow, a uniformed policeman.

"Watson, disperse this crowd."

"Yes, Lieutenant."

"Van Gelder," the lieutenant said, "care to let me in on what's going on here?"

"I don't know much more than you do, Lieutenant. This man—"

"Decker," Decker said.

"Yes, this man Decker claims one of my customers tried to kill him."

"Shot me in the back," Decker said.

"Is that right?" the lieutenant said.

"Somebody certainly shot him in the back," the doctor said, removing the table cloth, "as you can plainly see, Lieutenant."

"Hmm, yes," the lieutenant said.

Van Gelder was grey-haired, in his middle forties. He was about five eight, but solidly built. The lieutenant was in his late thirties, about six feet tall, with slicked back black hair, and a carefully trimmed mustache.

"This bullet is going to have to come out," the doctor said. "You'll have to come to my office. Do you feel strong enough to walk?"

"Yes."

"Mr. Decker, I'm Lieutenant Tennant."

Decker looked at the man to see if he was kidding, and the doctor muttered, "That's his name."

Decker supposed that it would only sound funny until the man made captain.

"Pleased to meet you."

"Do you know any reason why that man would want to shoot you in the back?" Tennant asked.

"Lieutenant, I've already told Mr. Van Gelder that I don't even know who the man was, let alone why he wanted to shoot me."

"Can't this wait?" the doctor asked.

"Very well. When you're finished with the doctor, Mr. Decker, I'd appreciate it if you came down to my office and made a statement—uh, if you're up to it, of course."

"In the morning," the doctor said. "He won't feel up to it until the morning."

"Very well, Doctor," Tennant said, "in the morning."

"Are you going to remove the dead man from my casino?" Van Gelder demanded. "I've got a business to run."

"That's already being taken care of, Van Gelder."

"Good."

"You can't go in there, miss," they heard the policeman on the door say.

"Get out of my way, I have business in there." Decker recognized Annie Tucker's voice.

"Tennant, for Christ's sake, tell your man to stand aside," Van Gelder said.

"Let her in, Watson."

"Yes sir," the policeman said, and dutifully stood aside.

Annie Tucker walked in and asked Decker, "How are you?"

"He'll be all right," the doctor said, "if I can ever get him to my office."

"Let's go," Decker said, standing up.

"Steady," the doctor said.

"Is this man a friend of yours?" Van Gelder demanded.

"Yes—no—I mean, he's a friend of Sally's."

"Your sister?"

"Yes." To the doctor she said, "Can I come along?"

"He might need someone to steady him."

"I'm strong enough," she said. In fact, Decker noticed that she had already fetched herself a wrap, so she had intended to go along, anyway.

"We're still open, Annie," Van Gelder said.

"I'll be back, Gerald."

She moved to Decker's side and put her arm around his waist. Her hair smelled extremely good.

"Who was your big friend?" he asked her.

"That was Sam Klingman."

"Klingman?" Van Gelder shouted. "Sam Klingman? He's one of my best customers. He loses a fortune in here every week. What happened to him?"

"He called out and saved my life," Decker said. "I'd like to thank him."

"You'll have time enough for that tomorrow," the doctor said. "If we don't get to my office soon—"

"All right, Doctor," Decker said. "We're going."

As they moved to the door the lieutenant said, "Remember, Mr. Decker. Tomorrow, my office."

And Van Gelder said, "Try not to be long, Annie. Remember, I'm still open."

Decker wondered what Van Gelder would say when he found the spot on his leather sofa where Decker had deliberately wiped his bloody hand.

Chapter Thirteen

The doctor had a carriage waiting outside which took them to his office. Annie Tucker waited in his outer office while the doctor laid Decker face down on a table in his examining room and removed the bullet.

"You're a good patient," he said afterward. "You barely made a sound."

"It's not the first time I've been shot," Decker said.

"Yes." the doctor said, casting his eyes over the scars already adorning Decker's body, "I can see that. This is fairly recent," he said, running his finger over a knife scar in Decker's side. It was recent enough that Decker moved away from the doctor's touch.

"Yes," he said.

"You apparently lead a violent life, Mr. Decker."

"Can I get up now?"

"I'd prefer you lie there a while, but it's up to you. You can rise if you like."

Decker sat up, wincing at the pain in his shoulder. The doctor had bandaged it tightly, and the bandage constricted his movements as he slid his shirt back on.

"My jacket?"

"The young lady has it in the other room."

"This suit was new," Decker said, mournfully.

"Better the suit than you, Mr. Decker."

"Yeah. What do I owe you, Doc?"

"The visit was to the Alhambra. They'll have to pay me."

"Will Van Gelder do that?"

"He'll bitch and moan," the doctor said, putting his instruments away, "but he'll do it."

"I'm much obliged to you, Doc."

"Don't mention it. Just get out of here so I can get to sleep."

"Right."

"And mind you, no sudden movements. You should stay in bed for two or three days, at the least, and a week if you know what's good for you."

"I'll keep that in mind. Thanks."

He went into the outer room, where Annie Tucker stood up, holding his jacket.

"It looks new," she said as she held it for him to slip on.

"It is—or was."

"Van Gelder will buy you a new one."

"Why?"

"Because you were shot in his place."

"He'll do that?"

"He won't like it, but he will. He wants to preserve his reputation. He's not the most pleasant of men, but he is a good businessman. It would be bad for business if something happened to you in his place and he didn't foot your bills. Where are you staying?"

Decker told her.

"I'll take you there."

"You don't have to—"

"We can share a cab," she said.

"All right."

They left, flagged a passing carriage, and gave the driver the location of Decker's hotel.

"Was that true?" she asked.

"What?"

"That you didn't know the man who shot you?"

"It was true."

"Why would a man you don't know try to shoot you?"

"It's been known to happen," Decker said. More and more, in fact. The more people he put away— or killed—the more there were walking around who would have liked to take revenge. Undoubtedly this man would turn out to be the brother or father—maybe even the husband—of someone Decker had once hunted and caught.

"You did Sally a good turn tonight. I appreciate it."

"She doesn't belong there."

"I should tell you to mind your own business, but you're right. She doesn't. It was the only place I could exert any pressure to get her a job."

"Have her come to my hotel in the morning and I'll get her a job."

"Doing what?"

"Anything but what she was doing tonight."

"You can do that?"

He nodded.

"My friend owns the place. He'll give her a job on my say-so."

"I . . . I don't know what to say."

He looked at her and said, "What about you?"

"What about me?"

"Would you want a job?"

"I've got one."

"Do you like what you're doing?"

"I don't know, but I've been doing it for three years, and I do it well."

"I can imagine."

"What does that mean?" she asked, sounding more amused than insulted.

"Oh, nothing."

"What did you and my sister talk about?"

"She . . . told me about home."

"Did she tell you the story about me taking the Tyler boys into the barn?"

"Uh, yes, she did."

Annie laughed.

"It's not true?"

"She heard that from Andy Tyler, and she believed him. She's very naive."

"I would say so. All the more reason why she shouldn't be working in a place like the Alhambra."

"I agree. If your friend can really give her a job, I'd be very grateful." She put her hand on his arm and squeezed it for emphasis.

"A simple thank you will do, Annie."

She pulled her hand away and said, "I'm sorry. Like I said, I've been at it for three years."

They rode the rest of the way in silence, and when they reached the Ballard House, she helped Decker get down.

"Don't forget to have Sally come by in the morning."

"You won't be up and around—"

"Just have her ask for me, or for Duke. I'll take care of it."

"All right. Thanks, Decker."

"Thank you, Annie, for your help tonight—and if you see Mr. Klingman—"

"I'll pass him the message. I'll be seeing you."

As she rode away in the carriage, Decker hoped that she was speaking the truth. He hoped that he *would* be seeing her—soon.

Chapter Fourteen

Duke came to see Decker early the next morning, letting himself in with his key.

"How did you sleep?"

Decker pushed himself painfully into a sitting position and said, "Lousy."

"Hurt?"

"Like hell."

The night before, when Decker had entered the lobby, he had stopped at the desk and asked for Duke. When Duke arrived in the lobby, he'd immediately noticed that something was wrong.

"Run into trouble?" he'd asked.

"Dissatisfied customer."

Duke called for help, and he and two other men had helped Decker to his room, and put him to bed.

Now Duke said, "I've ordered some breakfast brought up. You'll need to keep you strength up."

Decker started to argue that he wasn't hungry, but then simply nodded.

"You know, you should have let me get someone

to spend the night with you—you know, to take care of you."

"Like who?"

"Like Mona," Duke said. "The blonde with the braid."

"Oh, Mona. Well, Duke, I really didn't need any help."

"She could have taken your mind off of it."

"You ever been shot?"

"No."

"Takes more than even a pretty blonde to take your mind off of it."

"I'll take your word for it."

Decker swung his legs off the bed and put his feet on the floor.

"What are you doing?"

"I've got to go make a statement to the police."

"You can't—"

Decker stood up slowly, and then paused with his eyes closed when he was standing straight.

"Deck—"

"I also want to find out who I killed, Duke."

"I'll have the police come here to take your statement."

"Can you do that?"

Duke smiled.

"Without any problem. Who was the policeman there, last night?"

"Uh, Lieutenant . . . oh yeah, Tennant."

"Tennant?" Duke asked, smiling.

"Yeah. You know him?"

"I know him. Get right back into the bed. Your

breakfast will be here soon." Duke walked to the door and then said, "By the time you're done with it, Tennant will be here."

As Duke opened the door Decker called out, "Oh, by the way."

"What?"

"There's a young woman coming here this morning, name of Sally Tucker."

"What's she coming over for?"

"A job. I told her sister you'd hire her."

"Her, and the sister?"

"Just her, but the sister might come over with her."

"How will I know them?"

"You'll know them, especially if they're together."

"What can she do?"

"Ask her. She wasn't exactly suited to what she was doing at the Alhambra."

"She was working for Van Gelder?"

"Yeah."

"What does she look like?" Duke asked, with interest.

"Pretty, dark-haired—very dark hair—creamy skin—"

"Annie."

"What?"

"Sounds like Annie Tucker. Sure, I should have put that together when you said Sally Tucker."

"You know Annie Tucker?"

"Everyone knows Annie. She the woman who went to the doctor's with you?"

"Yes."

"And it's her sister who's coming here for a job?"

"That's right."

"I tell you," Duke said, looking excited, "if I could get Annie working here—but now, that'd never happen."

"Why not?"

"She belongs to Van Gelder."

"Belongs?"

"That's what I said," Duke said, opening the door. "Belongs. Lie back and relax. Breakfast will be here in minutes—and don't even think about getting out of that bed again. Not for a while."

"How do I eat?"

"Don't worry," Duke said, "I've taken care of everything."

After Duke left Decker closed his eyes and tried to will the stiffness out of his shoulders, and pain out of his wound. He wanted to get up and get dressed, but the simple act of standing up had him sweating. He was lucky that Duke had some influence with the police.

He wondered idly if Tennant was on Duke's payroll.

He wondered about the man he killed. He thought about Wesley Fairburn, the man he had killed in Evanville, Wyoming, last month. He was sure that both had died for the same cause—their unreasonable desire for revenge.

Fairburn had known he was in town, and had waited for a chance to face him.

The man last night couldn't have possibly known he was in town, so it must have been sheer coincidence that they were in the same place at the same time—and the man had recognized him.

Fairburn had chosen to take his revenge face to face, but the man last night had chosen to shoot him in the back. Luckily, the man had hurried his shot for some reason—perhaps nerves—giving Decker a chance to react. Had he been a man with steel nerves . . .

Realizing how close he had come to death made him shiver.

That was when he decided to get out of bed, after all. Even if it made his wound hurt like hell, the pain would remind him of something.

That he was still alive.

Chapter Fifteen

When the knock came at his door, Decker was dressed and on his feet. He actually felt much better being up and around.

When he answered the door he saw Mona, the braided blonde, standing there with a tray of food.

"Breakfast."

"Thanks, but—"

She walked past him and said, "Duke told me I wasn't to let you out of this room until you'd been fed."

"All right."

"He also asked me to change your bandage."

"You don't mind doing that?"

She grinned.

"I've changed plenty of bandages, Mr. Decker."

"I'll have to take my shirt off."

"That's no problem, and I have the fresh bandages right here on the tray."

"All right," Decker said, giving in, "let's get it done so I can eat and gain my release."

* * *

When Sally Tucker saw the Ballard House hotel, she felt that this would probably be more to her liking than the huge Alhambra, or any of the other hotels in Portsmouth Square.

She had mixed emotions about seeing Decker again, though. She was embarrassed about getting drunk on a glass of champagne, and yet she was grateful to him for not having taken advantage of her, and for arranging a job at the Ballard House.

She entered, walked to the desk tentatively, put her suitcase down, waited for the clerk to notice her, and then asked for either Decker or Duke Ballard.

When Duke saw the girl standing at the desk he knew she was Sally Tucker.

He knew she was Annie Tucker's sister, and that she would be as beautiful in a few years as her sister was now.

Maybe he didn't need Annie, after all.

"Miss Tucker?"

"Yes?" Sally said, turning away from the desk. The man she saw was just an inch or so taller than Annie was.

"I'm Duke Ballard, Decker's friend and the owner of this hotel."

"Oh, Mr. Ballard. I'm so grateful to you and Mr. Decker—"

"Is this yours?" he asked, indicating the bag.

"Yes."

"I'll have a man take it to your room."

"But—but you haven't hired me, yet."

"Decker wants me to hire you, Miss Tucker, then you're hired. It's just a question of *what* you'll be doing, and we can discuss that in my office."

"Is Decker all right?"

"He's fine," Duke said. "I'm sure he'll be down fairly shortly."

"What? Why, he was shot last night. He shouldn't be out of bed."

"Yeah, well," Duke said, taking her arm, "you tell him that when he comes down, huh? Let's see if he listens to you any better than he listens to me."

When Decker came down, moving gingerly so as not to jostle his shoulder, the clerk told him that Duke was in his office with Sally Tucker.

Decker went to the office, knocked on the door, and entered.

"Good morning, Sally," he greeted her.

She was seated in a chair in front of Duke's chair, and turned at the sound of his voice.

"Mr. Decker, you shouldn't be up."

"Where should I be?"

"In bed," she said, and then blushed.

Decker looked at Duke, and from the look on his friend's face he knew that Duke agreed with him. Sally Tucker did not belong in Portsmouth Square.

"We, uh, were just talking about my sister. Mr. Ballard—"

"Duke," Duke said, interrupting her.

"Duke was telling me that he knows Annie."

"Really?"

"I've tried to hire her away from Van Gelder

many times," Duke said, "but I can't match his . . . uh—"

"Salary?" Decker said.

"Exactly."

"Have you two decided what Sally will be doing?" Decker asked.

"She says she wouldn't mind waiting tables in the dining room."

"You have an opening?"

"We can make one. Of course, we have all waiters, so she'll be the only waitress."

"It'll bring more people in to eat," Decker said. "I'd much rather be waited on by a lovely woman than one of your homely waiters."

"Thanks."

"When can I start, Mr. Ball—uh, Duke."

"Today, if you like. Have you waited tables before?"

She hesitated before answering, "Some."

"Yeah, well, I'll have one of the boys show you along until you're ready."

"That would be fine!"

"I'll take you over there, then," Duke said, standing up.

"Your sister didn't come with you?" Decker asked.

"I'm afraid not, but she did say that I could do worse than work for Duke Ballard."

And she was right, too, Decker thought.

"That's nice of her . . . I think," Duke said.

Chapter Sixteen

They were crossing the lobby when a man both Decker and Duke recognized came through the front door.

It was Lieutenant Tennant.

He didn't look happy.

"That was fast," Decker said.

"I don't fool around," Duke said. "Want me to talk to him?"

"No, you've done enough. Take Sally into the dining room, I'll take care of the lieutenant."

"Fine. Use my office."

"Thanks."

Decker approached Tennant.

"I thought you'd be flat on your back," Tennant said. His tone plainly indicated that he was disappointed that Decker wasn't.

"I was, but I decided being on my feet would be healthier. The last thing I want to do is die in bed."

"Die? I didn't think your wound was—"

"It isn't. Come on, we can talk in the office."

Decker led the policeman to Duke's office, and

then lowered himself into Duke's chair behind the desk.

"You look stiff."

"A bullet will do that to you."

"I'll take your word for it."

"Haven't you ever been shot?"

Tenant looked uncomfortable, as if he was ashamed to admit he hadn't.

"No, never."

"Lucky man."

"I assume you've been shot at many times, given your occupation."

"Shot at, and shot," Decker said. "You checked me out?"

"I did. You're a bounty hunter."

"Guilty."

"Was there a bounty on that man last night?"

"Not that I know of, but if there was, I think I'd be entitled to collect, don't you?"

Tennant frowned.

"Did you identify him?"

"His name is Louis Jackman."

"Jackman," Decker repeated, "Jackman . . . of course. I brought in a Michael Jackman four years ago, or so."

"His father. He was hanged."

"He killed three men and a woman."

"I guess that didn't matter to Louis," Tennant said. He took out a pad and pencil and began asking questions.

Had Decker known that Jackman was in town? No.

Had Decker seen Jackman in the casino? No.

Was Decker here hunting anyone?

Decker lied. He said no.

"All right, I guess it was a coincidence that you were both in the same place together last night."

"I guess it was."

"That sort of thing must happen all the time to you, eh, Decker?" Tennant said, standing up.

"Sure, Lieutenant," Decker said. "All the time. I hope you'll forgive me if I don't stand up."

"No, I don't mind," Tennant said. He started for the door, then turned and faced Decker again with his hand on the door knob.

"I'll tell you what I do mind, though."

"What's that?"

"Being made to trot down here when you could have come to the office."

"Lieutenant, I didn't mean—"

"I don't care who Duke Ballard's friends are, Decker, don't ask him to have me come down here again. Understood?"

"Understood."

"Good—and try not to kill anyone else, huh?"

"I'll do my best."

Tennant left and Decker rested his head against the back of Duke's leather chair.

He fell asleep that way.

When Duke entered the room Decker opened his eyes immediately.

"That's it," Duke said, crossing the room. "You're going back to bed."

"No," Decker said, but he felt terrible. His mouth felt like the inside of one of his boots; his head throbbed; and his shoulder hurt like hell.

"Yes," Duke said. "Can we make it together or do we need help?"

Decker thought it over and then said, "I think we can make it."

"Well, let's give it a try."

Together they managed to get Decker to his room, where Duke deposited him on the bed.

"I don't do this for just anybody, you know," Duke said, pulling his friend's boots off.

"I love you, too, dear."

"Now lie back and rest, like the doctor said."

"How's Sally doing?"

"Fine. She's been here half an hour and she's already broken half a dozen dishes."

"I'll pay for them."

"Nobody asked you to. Are you gonna get some rest now?"

"I am a little sleepy," Decker admitted. "Maybe just a quick rest."

"Good. I'll check in on you later."

All Decker heard was, "Good, I'll check in . . ." and then he was asleep.

Chapter Seventeen

When Decker awoke he found Duke standing by the bed.

"Jesus," he said, "what time is it?"

"About eleven."

"That late?"

Duke shook his head.

"That early," he said. "It's eleven a.m., Deck. You slept all night."

"All night?" Decker said. "You mean all day and all night, don't you?"

"You needed it."

"You could have woke me."

"I was in here three times and you didn't move a muscle once."

"You came in here three times and I never woke up?" Decker asked in disbelief.

"That's right."

"Jesus," he said, rubbing his right hand over his face. "I'm dead three times."

"What?"

"In my business, I'd be dead three times if it wasn't you, Duke."

"But it was me, Deck. Believe me, nobody else could have gotten near your room. You needed the rest."

Duke may have been watching out for him while he slept, but that didn't make him feel any better. There was no excuse for sleeping that soundly, not after two attempts on his life within the past month.

"I've got to get up."

"How do you feel?"

"Fine."

Decker swung his legs around and put both feet on the floor. He stood up, waited a moment, and then repeated, "I feel fine."

"Yeah, well, a bath, a shave and some fresh clothes, and you may even look fine. Let's gather up some stuff and I'll take you downstairs."

They put together the items Decker needed, and then left the room. Decker walked most of the way without Duke's help, but accepted his arm on the stairs.

Decker bathed and dried himself, then pulled on his pants and called Duke in to bandage his wound. That done, he put on his shirt, his boots and then strapped on his gun.

"Now what?" Duke asked.

"Breakfast," Decker said. "I'm starved.

"I don't think I should do this to an injured man," Duke said in the dining room, "but our waitress is going to be Sally."

As if on cue Sally appeared to take their order.

"Hi, Sally," Decker said.

"Hello, Mr. Decker."

"Just call me Decker, Sally."

"All right, Mr.—I mean, Decker. What can I bring you?"

Decker ordered a huge breakfast consisting of eggs, steak, bacon, potatoes, biscuits, jam, and coffee.

"Duke?"

"Just some eggs, biscuits and coffee, Sally."

She gave them a sunny smile and said, "Coming right up."

"She fits in better here," Decker said.

"Tell that to my kitchen staff. She's almost single-handedly wiped us out of plates."

"Duke—"

Duke held up his hand and said, "I'm giving her a chance, Decker, but I'm warning you. By next week she might be a maid. At least she won't be able to break sheets and towels."

Sally managed to bring breakfast over to their table without dropping anything. Over breakfast Decker asked, "Have you heard anything about my girl."

"You still thinking about her? Jesus, Deck, give yourself time to recover. You've been shot, you know."

"I know. Anything?"

"No, nothing. If she's in town she's not working any kind of scam—yet."

"If she came here to spend the money, she won't be," Decker said.

"How will you find her, then?"

"By looking, Duke," Decker said, "just by looking."

"Yeah, well, maybe I should come with you," Duke said.

"Why?"

"Well, if the other night's any indication, you need someone to watch your back."

"I can watch my own back."

"Oh sure, you're doing a real good job of it."

There was an awkward moment of silence between them, and then Duke asked, "How often does this happen, Deck?"

"What?"

"The friend or a relative of someone you brought in trying to kill you?"

Decker hesitated, then said, "A lot more recently."

"Maybe it's time to move on to something else."

"Like what?"

"Another line of work."

"Name one."

"Part owner of a hotel."

Decker stared at Duke and saw that his friend was serious.

"That's a fine offer, Duke, but—"

"What offer? Am I offering it to you for nothing? I'm giving you the chance to buy your way in. You know, this place is growing."

"I appreciate it, I really do, but there's nothing else I'm cut out for, Duke. Believe me, I'd be a real terrible hotel owner."

"I tried," Duke said, spreading his arms. "What more can a friend do?"

"You can help."

"How?"

"Well, I don't think I want to take you away from here to watch my back, but you might be right about me needing someone. At least, until I'm fully healed."

Duke said, "Say no more, I've got just the fella in mind."

"Oh yeah? When can I meet him?"

"Later this afternoon. I'll get word to him and he'll be over."

"Just like that?"

Duke grinned and said, "He owes me a few favors."

"Is he any good?"

"Good enough."

"What's that mean?"

"You'll see."

Chapter Eighteen

At the same time, over in Portsmouth Square, Victor Van Gelder was having breakfast in his private suite with the beautiful Annie Tucker.

"Well, Annie, I understand your sister has left us," Van Gelder said.

"That's right, Victor," Annie Tucker said.

She had been to bed with Van Gelder the night before, but had returned to her own room to sleep. Now she sat across from him in his suite, wearing a filmy peignoir. He had sent Big Harry over to her room to "invite" her to breakfast.

"After one night? Don't tell me she didn't like it here."

"It just wasn't right for her, Victor."

"It's right for you, Annie."

"Sally and I are different."

"She's a beautiful young girl, Annie. Soon she may be as beautiful as you."

"Or more," Annie said. She wanted Van Gelder to know that there was no jealousy between the sisters. She didn't know what he was getting at.

"I was sort of counting on her to . . . do as good a job as you in the near future."

"I'm sorry, Victor, but she's just not cut out for this kind of work."

"I see." He picked up a muffin and began spreading jam on it. "Tell me, where did she go?"

"To another hotel."

"Here in the Square? Will they have her doing the same thing?"

"No, she went outside the Square."

"Outside," Van Gelder said, thoughtfully. "Where?"

"Victor, what does it matter—"

He brought his fist down on the table so hard that everything shook.

"Where?" he said, his tone calm.

"Ballard House."

"Duke Ballard's place?" he said. "You sent her there?"

"I didn't send there, Victor, she just . . . went."

"On her own."

"The man who was shot here the other night. He's a friend of Ballard's. He got her the job."

"Ah yes, your sister's friend. I paid his doctor's bill."

"He wasn't her friend. She didn't even know him until that night."

"And yet he got her a job?"

"Yes."

"He must have been a very satisfied customer."

"It wasn't like that."

He leaned over the table and said, "It is always like that, my dear Annie."

"Victor—"

"I don't think you should eat any more breakfast, Annie," Van Gelder said. "I think I noticed a few extra pounds on you last night. Not very becoming."

She stared at him, knowing he was baiting her.

"That's all right," she said, putting her napkin on the table. "I'm not very hungry, anyway."

"On your way out, please tell Harry I would like to see him."

She shuddered. "Big Harry," as the girls in the hotel called him, was the only man who had ever scared Annie Tucker. He was a huge man with sloping shoulders and arms knotted with muscle. It was generally known that Harry could have any girl in the hotel he wanted for the night, and that he was not called "Big" just because of his muscles. He had never had Annie because she was Van Gelder's girl, but she knew that if she ever fell out of favor with Van Gelder, he would toss her to Big Harry in a minute.

And Big Harry would love it.

She shuddered again and left the room.

When Big Harry Reno entered the suite, Van Gelder let him wait for a few minutes before speaking. It was Van Gelder's subtle way of reminding Harry who worked for whom.

"One of our girls has gone to work for Duke Ballard," he said.

"Sally," Harry Reno rasped.

"That's right," Van Gelder said, biting into a muffin smeared with jam. "I don't want any of the other girls thinking they can do the same."

"You want me to talk to them?"

"No," Van Gelder said, "I want something to happen at Ballard's place. I want that little toad to know that he can't hire girls away from me." Van Gelder looked at Reno and said, "Do I have to spell it out for you?"

"No, boss."

"Then do it."

"Sure, boss," Reno said, and left.

Van Gelder hated Duke Ballard. The man simply did not belong in San Francisco as the owner of a hotel, even one as insignificant as the Ballard House. The man had connections, though, a few friends high up. This time, however, he had gone too far.

And this time would be the last time.

After finding Harry and giving him Van Gelder's message Annie went to her room and got dressed.

She didn't like the way Van Gelder sounded when he was talking about her sister. She had to go to the Ballard House and warn Decker, Duke Ballard, and her sister to watch out for Van Gelder.

He was going to try something.

She was sure of it.

While Harry was still in Van Gelder's suite she made her way downstairs and left the hotel. The only person she saw on the way was Margot Winfield.

Margot wanted to be Victor Van Gelder's top girl and, for that reason, hated Annie Tucker.

"Going out, Annie?" Margot asked.

She was about Annie's age, and almost rivaled her beauty. She was a redhead, with a heart shaped face and a full bosom which she always showed off in extremely low-cut gowns.

"Just some early shopping, Margot."

"Sure, honey. You always go out this early to shop, don't you?"

Annie knew Margot would tell Van Gelder that she saw her leaving the hotel early, and she knew she'd have to be ready with a story—but that would come later.

Right now, she had to talk to Sally.

Victor Van Gelder listened with interest to what Margot Winfield had to tell him, and at the same time studied the girl. She was almost—and it was a big almost—as beautiful as Annie Tucker, and Van Gelder knew why she was telling him what she had seen.

He stood up from his table when she was finished and crossed the floor to stand before her.

"So you saw Annie leave the building early, eh?"

"Earlier than usual," Margot said, nodding her head, "a lot earlier."

"And you think this is significant?"

"I wouldn't have told you otherwise, Mr. Van Gelder," the girl said, solemnly.

He put his hand to her face, touched the soft skin with his fingers. She was about to lean into his touch when he pulled the hand away, and then slapped her across the cheek hard enough to leave the red imprint of his hand.

"Mr. Van Gelder!" she screamed, putting her hand to her burning cheek. "I don't understand. What—"

"That's for not following her and seeing where she went," Van Gelder told her gently. "You must learn, Margot, if you're going to bring me information, bring me something I can use."

"Yes sir," she said, rubbing her cheek. Her eyes were wet with tears, but she didn't cry. She had spunk.

"All right, Margot, get out."

"I'll remember next time—"

"Get out!"

She jumped, then turned and rushed out the door.

Van Gelder clasped his hands behind his back. Annie could have simply been going shopping, but Van Gelder had slept with her enough times to know that she was not an early person. She rarely left the hotel before noon.

What had changed her mind, today?

Chapter Nineteen

Decker and Duke were finishing up breakfast when the desk clerk came in and stopped by their table.

"Yes, Arthur?" Duke said.

"There is a lady at the desk, sir, asking to see either you or Mr. Decker."

"Well, bring her in, Arthur. Don't keep a lady waiting in the lobby."

"Yes sir."

As Arthur left Decker wrinkled his nose in distaste and said, "Why do you hire people like that?"

"What's wrong with Arthur."

"Nothing, if you like men who smell sweeter than most women you know."

"He's good at his job," Duke said. "As long as that holds true, I don't much care what he smells like."

"It's your hotel."

Arthur came back with the lady, who turned out to be Annie Tucker.

"Well," Duke said, rising, "this is a pleasure. Hello, Annie."

"Duke," she said.

"Forgive my loutish friend for not rising, but he's a little under the weather, as you know."

She looked at Decker and asked, "How are you feeling?"

"Much better."

"That's good. May I join you gentlemen?"

"Of course," Duke said, pulling a chair out for her and holding it. "Can I get you some breakfast?"

"No, thanks, I've already had some. Is Sally around?"

"She's waiting tables this morning."

Annie made a face, then sighed and said, "Well, I suppose she is better suited to this."

"What brings you here today, Annie?" Decker said.

A worried look came over her face.

"I came to warn you."

"About what?" Decker asked.

"Not what, my friend," Duke said, "who." He looked at Annie and said, "Van Gelder, right?"

"Yes. He's very upset that you've hired one of his girls away from him."

"One of his girls?" Duke said. "She worked there one night."

"That's all it takes," Annie said. "Oh, I never should have let her come here."

"If you knew he'd be upset, why *did* you let her come here?" Decker asked.

"Because I was thinking of her," Annie said.

"What's Van Gelder got in mind?" Duke asked.

"I don't know," she said, shaking her head. "but after he talked to me he called for Big Harry?"

"What's a Big Harry?" Decker asked.

"Harry Reno," Duke said. "He's an ex-fighter that Van Gelder uses to scare people."

"He does more than just scare people," Annie said. "Sometimes he breaks them."

"He wouldn't just send him over here to start trouble, would he?" Decker asked.

"No, but he'd give him his head," Duke said. "This is not your run of the mill, punched out boxer we're talking about. Harry may be big, but he's got a brain. That's why he got out of the game while he still had it."

"What would he try?"

Duke shrugged.

"I guess we'll have to wait and see."

"You'll have to protect Sally—" Annie started to say, but at that moment Sally herself came walking over to the table.

"Hi, Annie!" she said, happily.

"Hello, darling," Annie Tucker said. She rose and embraced her sister. Decker didn't have any siblings, but he could see that Annie and Sally Tucker truly loved each other. "How are they treating you here?"

"Oh, everyone is wonderful," Sally said. "Duke is so patient."

"What's a few broken dishes," Duke said with a wave of his hand.

"Come on, I'll show you around," Sally said. She looked at Duke then and said, "May I?"

"Sure. Maybe your sister will like it here and come to work, too."

"Oh, that would be wonderful," Sally said.

"Come on, darling. Let's talk," Annie said, and the two women walked away arm in arm.

"Do we have to get our own coffee, now?" Decker asked.

"Hey, you're sitting with the boss," Duke said, frowning.

"What does that mean?"

"It means I'll get up and get it myself."

When Duke returned with a new pot of coffee Decker asked, "Have you got much help around here?"

"If you mean your kind of help, I can get it."

"I think you'd better. What's going on between you and Van Gelder?"

"We don't like each other. It's as simple as that."

"Nothing is ever simple, Duke, especially where you're concerned."

Duke grinned and said, "Remind me to tell you about it sometime. Meanwhile, let's finish this coffee and then I can go out and round up a few good hands, along with the man I promised you to watch your back."

"We may have to put that off for a while," Decker said.

"Why?"

"Because, my friend," Decker said, "I think you may need somebody around to watch *your* back, for a while."

Chapter Twenty

Decker spent the afternoon in his room, napping. When he awoke he felt strong enough to go for a walk.

Walking around San Francisco was an experience, mostly because there were so many people, and so many different types of stores and buildings. Decker didn't really pay much attention to them, though. He was thinking about women; about Sally Tucker, and Annie Tucker, the poker playing Stella Morrell and, ultimately, the con woman with no name but many faces. Somehow, he'd gotten way off the trail and involved in things other than hunting her down . . . or was he deliberately avoiding the hunt?

That had never happened to him before. "The hunt" had always stirred his blood, made him feel alive. Could it be different this time because he was hunting a woman? A woman whose only crime was that she had bilked banks and other establishments out of money they could probably well afford? After all, she hadn't killed anyone.

His thoughts strayed to Annie Tucker. She did not seem happy working for Van Gelder, so why did she? If she could see that it was not right for her sister, then why couldn't she see the same thing for herself?

Decker wasn't paying attention when the woman stopped out of a hat shop and almost into his path, but he managed to avoid a collision through instinct.

"I'm sorry—" the woman started to say, and then he saw that it was Stella Morrell.

"Hello, Stella."

"Hello, Decker. I heard about your . . . how are you feeling?"

"Fine. I thought a walk would do me good."

"I thought some shopping would do me some good. Relax me. Things haven't exactly been going well at the game."

"I'm sorry."

She shrugged.

"A run of bad luck. I'll ride it out."

"Are you going back to the hotel?" Decker asked.

"Yes."

"Do you mind if I walk with you?"

"Why . . . no, I don't mind."

"I thought we might talk about this person you're looking for."

Her eyes widened.

"Really?"

"I can't promise anything, you understand, but I'm willing to listen."

"That's all I ask."

"Well, let's walk and talk, then."

They walked, but Stella Morrell did all of the talking.

The person she wanted to hire Decker to find was her sister. It seemed that her younger sister had married back east, in Chicago—which was where Stella was from—and Stella had been receiving letters from their mother about wedding preparations, and then about the wedding, and later about the marriage.

"Recently, I received a letter from my mother telling me that my sister's marriage had broken up . . . because she had caught her husband cheating on her."

"That's a rough break."

"You don't know how rough. She killed him, Decker," Stella said as they reached the hotel, "she shot him and his lover and killed them both."

"It must have been terrible for her."

"Mother says she disappeared after that, afraid that the police would be after her, or simply ashamed to show her face."

"Your mother has no idea where she might have gone?"

"West, that was all mother's letter said. She thought that perhaps she was coming west to try and find me."

"I'm afraid there's not much I could do in a case like this, Stella. For one thing, I'd have to start my search from Chicago, and I just don't have the time—"

"I understand," she said, touching his arm, "I really do. It was silly of me to ask."

"No, it wasn't silly, and I can certainly keep my eyes open for her. What does she look like?"

"I haven't seen her in five years, since she was seventeen, but even then she was a beauty. She'd wear her hair long, because she loved it that way. It's auburn."

She went on to give Decker some idea of what her sister might look like now. About five four, slim, but with a good figure.

"Do you think she might have come this far west?" he asked her.

"Well, I spend a lot of time in San Francisco, and usually at this hotel. I've written mother to tell her that, in case my sister gets in touch with her."

"How long has she been missing?"

"Almost a year."

"And has your mother hired anyone to find her? Detectives?"

"No. My mother is afraid that if a detective finds her, he'll turn her over to the police."

"That's possible."

Stella looked concerned all of a sudden and said, "You wouldn't feel compelled to do that, would you, Decker? If you found her?"

"If I found her I'd tell her where she could find you, Stella. The two of you could work it out from there."

Stella breathed a sigh of relief.

They entered the hotel and went up the stairs together to the second floor. Stella's room was on the third floor, while Decker had the largest suite on the second.

"Well, thanks for listening, Decker."

"I'm sorry about before—" he began.

"Don't be sorry. I shouldn't have gotten so angry."

"Good luck with the game."

He watched as she began to ascend to the third floor, then called out, "Stella!"

She turned to look at him.

"You haven't told me the most important thing."

"What's that?"

"Your sister's name."

"Oh, silly me," she said. "It's Julie, Julie Morrell. Well, it was Julie Morrell," she amended. "Her married name is Landan, Julie Landan."

Chapter Twenty-one

Julie Landan looked around her lavish hotel room and thought, this is the life. This is what I'm entitled to, what I should have.

She'd been there for five days, but she got the same feeling every time she walked into the room. It was a feeling of wonder that there were people in the world who actually lived this way all of the time.

That was her ultimate goal, then, to live this way all the time. What she needed to make that work was one huge con, where she'd make so much money she could retire.

It had never occurred to her early in her life that she'd be making the best living as a con woman, but she felt certain once she had put her mind to it, she was the best there was.

She looked at the new dresses she had laid out on the bed and wondered which one she should wear tonight. There were three men who had approached her over the past five days, and although she had not slept with any of them, she had managed to keep them interested. She had to find which one was was the richest. She didn't usually work cons on individuals, but it had occurred to her since her arrival in San Francisco that there were individual men who were even more wealthy than banks and other institutions.

She decided on the blue dress, low cut but tasteful. She did not want to be mistaken for one of the prostitutes working the hotel.

She decided to spend the day shopping. She had enough money to live this way for another week or so. After that, if she hadn't found "Mr. Right," she could always go on to the next bank on her list.

Not once did it occur to her that someone might be on her trail.

Chapter Twenty-two

Instead of going to his room, Decker decided to look for Duke. He went back down the stairs—slowly, but firmly—and was surprisd to see Annie Tucker in the lobby, apparently getting ready to leave. She saw him and waited while he approached her.

"I'm surprised you're still here," he said. "Must have been a long visit."

"I felt I owed Sally that," Annie said. "I haven't spent much time with her since her arrival in San Francisco, and she did come here to be with me. I—I apologized for putting her in an awkward position the other night."

"If she came here to be with you, it sounds like she should be living with you."

"I'd like that, I really would," Annie said, and Decker believed her, "but it's not possible."

"Van Gelder wouldn't approve, eh?"

"Especially with her working over here."

"What would he do if you came to work over here?"

She laughed and said, "Doing what? Waiting tables?"

"You could do the same thing you're doing at the Alhambra."

"With Duke Ballard taking Van Gelder's place?"

"Only as your employer."

Her eyes narrowed for a moment and then she asked, "Do you have a piece of this place? Maybe you're the one who would replace Van Gelder."

"I'm not looked to replace anyone, Miss Tucker," he said, "and I was offered a piece of this place, but turned it down."

"Why?"

"It's not my style."

"What is your style?"

"It's not San Francisco."

"Then why are you here?"

"I'm . . . looking for someone."

"Who?"

"A woman."

She laughed.

"Plenty of those around here."

"A particular woman."

"A lot of them are particular—all right, I'm sorry. Maybe I can help. What's her name?"

"I don't know her name—but there is someone else I'd like to ask you about."

"Who?"

"Have you met anyone named Julie Landan?"

"Landan? Not that I know of. She's not the one you're looking for?"

"No, her sister is looking for her—much the way Sally came looking for you, I guess."

"And this woman you're looking for—what do you want with her?"

"She's got a price on her head."

"Ah hah," Annie said, as if she understood. "You're a bounty hunter."

"That's right."

"Hunting people down for money is your style."

It was a harsh way of putting it, but he certainly couldn't deny it.

"That's right."

"That sort of makes you just as much a whore as I am, doesn't it?"

It was an observation made on her part, without rancor, and again he found that he couldn't really disagree.

"I guess so."

"Sorry I can't help you."

"That's all right," he said. "I'm used to doing things on my own."

"I have to get back," she said. She started for the door, then stopped. "That shooting the other night. What was that about?"

Decker shrugged and winced with pain.

"Just somebody's son—or brother—out for revenge."

"That must happen a lot, in your business."

"More and more, lately."

"Sounds like you're the one who needs a career change."

"I'll consider it."

"See you around," she said, and left.

Tough lady, he thought, tough and beautiful. Too good for the likes of Van Gelder.

Decker turned away from the door and saw Sally Tucker enter the lobby from the dining room. She saw him and hurried over to him.

"Oh, Decker, I can't thank you enough for this job. Everyone is so nice."

"I'm glad you're happy."

"There's only one thing that could make me happier."

"What's that?" he asked, although he thought he already knew.

"Getting Annie away from that terrible Mr. Van Gelder."

"What makes you think he's so terrible."

"Do you know what he wanted me to do when I started working for him?"

"What?"

"He wanted me to have—to sleep with him."

"He didn't."

"Yes, he did, and all the while he's sleeping with my sister. That's a terrible man, Decker."

"It sure is."

"And he has Annie working as a—a—"

"Prostitute."

"Yes."

"Seems to me she could leave if she wanted to."

"He has some sort of hold over her," Sally said, leaning forward and lowering her voice.

"Maybe she just likes living high," Decker said.

"Duke certainly couldn't give her all the things Van Gelder does."

"Annie has always liked spending money, but I don't think that's it. I think he has a hold over her. If only—"

"If only what?" he asked, feeling as if this innocent little girl was suckering him into something.

"If only someone could find out what it was."

"Whoa!" he said. Everybody wanted to drag him into *their* problems, while he had plenty of problems of his own. "Sally—"

"Couldn't you try, Decker?"

"Sally, I'm not a detective—"

"Duke says you're very good at what you do."

"Duke said—"

"And Annie said she thought you were a very dangerous man to be around."

"That's probably just because people like shooting at—"

"Decker," Sally said, putting her hand on his arm, "I'd be ever so grateful."

From another woman—Stella, or even her own sister, Annie—that statement would have meant something else, entirely. From Sally, it simply meant that she would be just that, *grateful*.

"Sally—" he said, looking into her wide, pleading, innocent eyes, "Sally—I'll see what I can do."

"Oh, Decker," she said, squeezing his arm, "you're not dangerous at all. You're very nice."

"Yeah, that's me," he said, "nice Decker."

"I have to get back to work now. I'll see you later."

"All right."

He watched her hurry back to the dining room, and spotted Duke coming from the direction of his office. He moved to intercept him.

"Was that Sally you were talking to?" Duke asked.

"Yes, and Annie before that, and Stella before that."

"Popular man."

"Everybody wants me to solve their problems—except Annie."

"Hers are probably the most serious."

Decker told Duke what Sally said about Van Gelder having a hold over Annie, and asked him for his opinion.

"I wouldn't doubt it, Decker. That's the way it works, here. You need somebody, you get something on them."

"You mean like you and Tennant?"

Duke grinned.

"Someday I'll tell you what I have on him."

"And how you got it."

Duke grinned again.

"What about Van Gelder, Duke? What could he have on Annie that would make her stay there, whore for him and sleep with him?"

"Listen," Duke said, "he may have something on her that makes her stay with him, but take my word for it, Annie Tucker is too good at what she does not to like it . . . a little."

"Maybe . . ."

"What's Stella want you to do?"

"Find her sister."

"Ah . . . I didn't even know she had one. What's her story?"

"I'll keep that one to myself for a while, Duke, if you don't mind."

"Personal, huh?"

"Yeah."

"All right, I won't try to drag it out of you. Listen, there's someone coming over here who I want you to meet."

"Who?"

"I'll tell you when he gets here. Be in my office in an hour, okay?"

"Sure."

Duke started away, then stopped and asked, "How's your shoulder?"

"Fine."

"Yeah, I can see that. You always move like you been dragged a hundred yards behind a horse."

"Tell me something."

"What?"

"How tight a hold do you have on Tennant."

"Why?"

Decker shrugged.

"You never know when you'll need a favor from a policeman."

"I can probably get you a favor done—depending on what it is."

"I'll let you know."

"Okay. Remember, one hour in my office."

"I'll be there."

Decker decided to spend the hour in his room,

resting. His shoulder felt pretty good, but there was no point in pushing it. The time for pushing it would come soon enough, and he wanted to be in shape for it.

Chapter
Twenty-three

Fifty-nine minutes later Decker knocked on the door of Duke's office and entered. Duke was seated behind his desk, and another man was sitting in a straight backed chair in front of the desk.

"Decker, I want you to meet Johnny Bendix. Johnny, this is Decker."

Bendix stood, and Decker saw a tall, powerfully built man in his twenties. He wore a well cared for Remington revolver on his hip.

"Decker," Bendix said, inclining his head in greeting.

"Bendix."

"I've heard of you," Bendix said.

"Oh?"

"I've heard you're good. I'm wondering why Duke needs me when he's got you around."

"Why don't you ask Duke?"

Bendix turned halfway so that he could see Duke and still keep an eye on Decker. He was a cautious man.

"Decker's a friend, Johnny," Duke said. "You, you're hired help."

That was putting it bluntly, and Bendix seemed to accept that as an answer.

"In addition," Duke said, "you're not here to help me, you're here to help Decker."

"I see," Bendix said. He looked at Decker and said, "You're carrying some lead."

"An ounce or so."

"I guess a man in your line of work could use somebody to watch your back."

"Not usually, but San Francisco's a little crowded. Lots of places for back-shooters to jump in and out of."

"You got that right," Bendix said. He looked at Duke and said, "Whose payroll am I on?"

Before Decker could answer Duke said, "Mine. Usual arrangements."

"Good enough." Bendix looked at Decker again and said, "I'm all yours."

"That thought makes me all warm inside. There's something else you should know."

"What?"

"We may be crossing paths with Van Gelder."

"And Big Harry," Duke added.

Bendix considered the information for a moment, then shrugged and said, "Let's up the price a bit and I'm still yours."

"Done," Duke said.

"What about you?" Decker asked Duke.

"I've taken three more men on as extra security.

Danny Peoples, Sam Mitchum and Carlos Caliente."

Decker looked at Bendix who said, "Good men, all of them."

"If Van Gelder wants to get in here to start something, he's going to have to get by them."

"Work for hire?" Decker asked.

"Sure."

"What if Van Gelder offers to pay them more?" Decker asked.

"The same thing would happen if Van Gelder offered me more money," Bendix said.

"What's that?" Decker asked.

"They'd say no. Once they take on a job they work for the man who hired them, same as me."

"Why's that?"

"If word gets around that you can be bought off, you're out of business."

The logic made sense.

"All right then," Decker said, "let's go."

"Where?"

"We might as well start at the top," Decker said.

"Van Gelder?" Duke asked.

"Right."

Bendix shook his head and said, "You ain't gonna make this an easy job, are you?"

Chapter Twenty-four

With Johnny Bendix at his back Decker went over to the Alhambra and informed the clerk behind the desk that he wanted to see Van Gelder.

"*Mister* Van Gelder is busy right now, sir," the prissy clerk said. All the desk clerks in San Francisco seemed prissy and sweet smelling.

"Well, tell him I'm here."

"I'm afraid I can't do that, sir."

"Listen—"

"Excuse me," Bendix said to Decker. "Duke said you shouldn't exert yourself."

"Breaking this fella's arm wouldn't be any exertion at all, Johnny."

"Still and all," Johnny Bendix said, "I think I should break his arm."

"If you'll wait here," the clerk said, hurriedly, "I'll tell Mr. Van Gelder that you are here." He came around the desk and virtually ran across the lobby.

"You and I are gonna work together real fine," Johnny said, grinning.

"That all depends," Decker said.

"On what?"

"Which arm were you going to break?"

They waited for the clerk to return, and when he did he had another man in tow.

"That's Mark Sideman," Bendix said, "Van Gelder's right hand man."

"I thought Big Harry was Van Gelder's right hand man."

"Big Harry," Bendix said, "is Van Gelder's fist."

"Can I help you gentlemen?" Sideman asked as the clerk scurried back around behind the desk.

"I'd like to see Van Gelder."

"*Mister* Van Gelder is busy, at the moment," Sideman said. Van Gelder had his staff well trained.

"That's what this prissy dude behind the desk said," Decker said.

"Yes, and you proceeded to threaten him. Would you like to threaten me?"

"Of course not—"

"I would," Bendix said, grinning wolfishly.

Sideman was Bendix's height and age, but he was a lot slimmer, and didn't seem to have the physical ability to stand up to Bendix. Still, he returned Bendix's look and said, "No, you wouldn't. You're Bendix, aren't you?"

"That's right."

"Seems to me you've done some work for us."

"I've worked for *Van Gelder* on occasion," Bendix said. "I've never worked for you, Sideman. You couldn't afford me."

"Are you working for this gentleman, now?"

"No," Bendix said, and did not elaborate.

"Are you prepared to leave without seeing Mr. Van Gelder?" Sideman asked Decker.

"No."

"I might be able to get him to see you . . . alone."

"No," Decker said, shaking his head. "It doesn't work that way. He'll see both of us."

"And why will he?"

"Because you'll ask him to, and he'll say yes."

Sideman stared at Decker, as if he were trying to decide something.

"Go on," Decker said, "ask him."

Sideman sighed and said, "Wait here."

He turned and left and Bendix looked at the clerk, who tried to find something to occupy him.

"You're pushing hard," Bendix said.

"Van Gelder will respond to that."

"I'll bet you a beer he doesn't see us."

"You're covered."

Sideman returned approximately five minutes later and said, "Follow me, please."

"Both of us?" Bendix asked.

"Both of you."

"Well," Bendix said, "I'll be damned."

Apparently, Van Gelder did his business in his two room suite, and when they entered behind Mark Sideman, he was either having a late lunch or an early dinner.

"Bendix!" Van Gelder said when he saw the other man.

"Van Gelder."

Later, Decker would have to ask Bendix about

his relationship with Van Gelder. Or better yet, ask Duke about it.

Van Gelder recovered from his obvious surprise at seeing Johnny Bendix and fixed his gaze on Decker.

"Mr. Decker. I trust you are recovering from your unfortunate mishap the other night."

"I'm getting along."

"What can I do for you?"

"I wanted to thank you for covering my medical bill."

Van Gelder had picked up his fork and now he put it down again.

"Excuse me, but my information is that you used some strong-arm tactics and threats to get in to see me. I'm sure it must have been about something more important than medical bills."

"No," Decker said. "That's it. I like to say my thanks in person."

Van Gelder frowned.

"You have no other business?"

"No," Decker said, "that is, unless you have some with me."

"No, no," Van Gelder said, "nothing."

The man was obviously puzzled, which is what Decker wanted to accomplish.

"We'll be leaving, then," Decker said.

"Mark, show these gentlemen out."

"We can find our way," Decker said, moving towards the door. "Thanks, anyway. Come on, Johnny."

Decker went through the door with Bendix on

his heels. Out in the hall Bendix said, "I don't know about him, but you sure have got me confused."

"Him, too, Johnny."

"Is that all you wanted to do?"

"That's all," Decker said. "Just make him think a little."

Bendix shook his head and followed Decker down to the lobby and out.

"I didn't see Big Harry," Decker said.

"Believe me, Decker, you don't want to see Big Harry. Take my advice about him. If you see him, shoot first and ask questions later."

After they had left Portsmouth Square Decker said, "You want to tell me about you and Van Gelder?"

"What's to tell. I've done some work for him."

"I wish you had told me that before."

"Duke knew," Bendix said. "Hell, Decker, I've worked for half the hotel owners in this town, and will probably work for the other half before I'm through. I'm good at what I do and they all know it."

"Van Gelder seemed more than a little surprised."

"I admit that Van Gelder tends to think in more permanent terms than most of the others."

"Meaning?"

"Meaning I've done enough work for him from time to time that he obviously thinks he owns me."

"And he doesn't?"

"Nobody does," Bendix said, his tone cold. "I do a job for money, same as you."

"All right," Decker said.

"All right," Bendix echoed. "What's next?"

"Later tonight we'll visit some of the other hotels. I'm looking for someone."

"Who?"

"A woman."

"What's her name?"

"I don't know."

"What's she look like?"

"I'm not sure."

"Jeez," Bendix said, "that shouldn't be no trouble at all, huh?"

When they reached the hotel Decker asked Bendix, "Do you have a suit?"

"Hey, I live in this town, don't I?" Bendix asked. "Of course I have a suit."

"Come back later, and be wearing it."

"I don't have to come back," Bendix said.

"Why not?"

"Duke gave me a room in the hotel."

Decker wondered how Duke made any money if he was always giving away rooms.

"All right, then meet me in the lobby at eight and we'll hit some of the other hotels in the Square.

"I'll be there."

As they went past the front desk the clerk said, "Mr. Decker?"

"Yeah?"

"Mr. Ballard wanted me to tell you that he's waiting in your room for you."

"What for?"

The clerk shurgged, but then added, "I did notice that he had his tailor with him."

"Tailor?" Bendix said, laughing. "And you asked me if I had a suit?"

"Mine has a bullet hole in it," Decker said.

"Well, let's hope we can avoid having that little problem again."

"Amen."

"The tailors in this town are thieves!"

Chapter Twenty-five

"Mr. Decker?"

"Yeah?"

"Could you move a little to your left, please?"

"Is this thing going to be ready by tonight?" Decker asked Duke.

"Of course," Duke said, but Decker noticed the outraged look on the face of the tailor, a small, pudgy man with surprisingly graceful fingers. "My man is the best."

"I hope so."

"Stand still, please!" the tailor said.

Decker frowned, but stood still.

"How did it go at Van Gelder's?" Duke asked.

"I don't think he likes me."

"Small loss."

"He also didn't like the idea that Johnny Bendix was with me. You didn't tell me that Bendix worked for Van Gelder."

"Bendix works for anyone who'll pay him. He's worked for Van Gelder before, and he's worked for me and a lot of others. He's loyal, though, to the one he's working for at the moment."

"So I understood."

"What do you think of him?"

"He's smart, and he's got good instincts. Is he any good with that gun?"

Duke nodded.

"And with his hands. He'll watch your back about as well as it's ever been watched, Decker."

"I hope so."

"Where are you going tonight?"

"Just going to hit some of the hotels in the Square, see if I can spot anybody."

"I still don't see how you can hope to find someone when you don't even know what she looks like."

"I'm not completely in the dark."

"Oh no?"

"Well, you saw the drawings on the poster. There is a similarity among them all."

"Around the eyes, yes, but you forget what women can do to their eyes with makeup, you know. Probably change the entire shape of them. Besides, you'd have to be real observant to even notice."

"And I'm not?"

"That's not what I meant."

"What did you mean?"

"I don't know what I meant," Duke said. "I just wish you'd forget your business and come and join me in mine."

"There!" the tailor said.

"Done?" Decker asked.

"Finally."

"All right. Let me get this off and you can get it ready by tonight . . . right?"

The tailor looked at Duke, and then said, "Right."

Decker removed the suit, gave it to the tailor and saw him to the door. Then he turned and addressed himself to Duke's last remark.

"I told you before, Duke, I appreciate the offer, but the hotel business is not for me."

"Why not? Lots of good-looking women, good food, nice place to live—"

"You've got to stay in one place."

Duke stared at his friend and then said, "Yeah, I can see how that would be a drawback for you."

"Well, now that we agree on that, why don't you get out and let me get some rest. I'm going to have a late night, tonight."

"How's the shoulder?"

"A little rest would help."

"Okay, okay, I'm going."

"Will you be dealing tonight?"

"Yes, why?"

"Just like to know where you'll be in case I need you."

"I'll be dealing. The game's starting to get interesting. Maybe you'll have time to sit in again before it's over."

"We'll see," Decker said.

As Duke left, Decker relaxed on the bed. Sitting in on a poker game, where he would more than likely be cleaned out, was the furthest thing from his mind.

Chapter Twenty-six

Julie Landan was resting on her bed. She'd had a full afternoon of shopping, and had returned to her hotel exhausted. She didn't know how rich men's wives managed to do this every day.

Johnny Bendix spent the afternoon in the Ballard Hotel saloon, playing low-stakes poker and drinking beer. He had found the morning with Decker interesting, and was looking forward to seeing the man in action that evening.

Toward late afternoon, he picked out one of the girls who worked the saloon and took her up to his room.

After all, it was all free.

Annie Tucker was nervous.

She knew that Margot had told Van Gelder that she'd left the hotel early that morning, and yet the whole afternoon had passed without Van Gelder calling for her.

What did he have up his sleeve?

She thought about Big Harry and shuddered.

She was glad she'd gotten Sally away from Van Gelder, whatever it might cost her.

On one hand, Sally Tucker was happy, and on the other, she was not.

She was glad that she had a nice job in a good hotel with pleasant people to work with, but she was still worried about her sister, working at the Alhambra for Van Gelder.

She hoped that Decker would be able to help Annie, the way he had helped her.

Van Gelder sat in his room, watching Margot as she slept on his bed. The sheet was on the floor and she was naked. Her skin was very pale, and she had big breasts that barely flattened out when she lay on her back. She was eager to please, uninhibited and inventive in bed.

Still, she wasn't Annie Tucker.

He stroked his jaw and wondered about his feelings for Annie. They were stronger than he liked to think, but if he let her get away with making a fool of him, he'd be the laughingstock of San Francisco.

Maybe he'd give her one more chance.

Just one.

Big Harry sat in the dining room of the Alhambra Hotel. He knew that Van Gelder wouldn't be pressing him for his plan concerning the Ballard House, but he was in a hurry to get the job done, anyway. That's why he was annoyed that Ballard had put on extra security—and they were good boys, too.

Well, he'd gotten some good boys of his own.

Three of them were seated at the table with him, and he was buying them drinks.

"What's the job, Harry?" Seidl asked.

"The Ballard Hotel."

"What do you want done to it?" Murphy asked.

"Go and have some dinner," Harry said, "maybe do some gambling. Complain about the service."

"How hard do you want us to complain?" Palmer asked.

Harry gave them all long stares and said, "Hard."

Mark Sideman thought that Victor Van Gelder was ready to be taken.

He'd been working for the man for two years, getting paid less than he was worth, taking all the shit Van Gelder threw his way, watching and waiting for a sign of weakness—and now he'd seen it.

Annie Tucker.

Wasn't it always a woman?

Walking past the dining room Sideman saw Harry talking to three men. Van Gelder had probably made some arrangements with Harry for a job, and kept Sideman ignorant of it.

Sideman was supposed to be Van Gelder's business manager, but he didn't like being kept out of the rest of Van Gelder's business affairs. He thought he deserved better.

And by God, he was going to get it.

Chapter Twenty-seven

When Decker got down to the lobby, Bendix was already waiting, looking remarkably resplendent in a black suit, similar to the one Decker was wearing. He wondered if Bendix had been to see Duke's tailor.

"Do you have a gun?" Decker asked.

Bendix held back the left side of his jacket to show Decker the shoulder rig. Decker himself was wearing the shoulder rig that Duke had given him, but recalling the way the gun had snagged on his suit jacket the night of the shooting, he had made a few trial runs with it in his room before leaving.

"You fellas look like a couple of high rollers," Duke said, coming up behind them.

"Might get lucky," Bendix said.

"You never know," Decker said.

"You never know," Duke agreed.

"Have you got your extra security on tonight?" Decker asked.

"Sure. Why? You expecting anything, tonight?"

Decker shrugged.

"Tonight's as good a night as any. Just have them keep their eyes open."

"They will. I'll be around, too. I decided to have someone else deal tonight."

"Well, watch your step."

"I was just going to tell the two of you the same thing."

Portsmouth Square was packed with hotels that were also gambling houses. The Parker House, the El Dorado, the Empire, the St. Charles and the Varsouvienne were just a few of them.

Decker chose the Parker House as their first stop of the night. Bendix entered first, followed by Decker. Bendix would stand at a roulette table, or a blackjack table, and Decker would move about the room. When Bendix received a nod from Decker he would move into the dining room, again followed by Decker.

In leaving the hotel they did it the opposite way. Decker would leave the dining room first, followed by Bendix, and they'd move out of the gambling casino in the same manner, just in case there was someone there who recognized Decker and harbored some ill will.

After the Parker House they went to the El Dorado, and then to the Verandah, which featured as its entertainment a one-man band. The man blew a set of pipes that were tied to his chin while he beat a drum on his back with a set of sticks that were fastened to his elbows. He held a pair of cymbals in his hands, and stomped the floor with his feet. He was certainly not artistic, but he was energetic and loud.

The Bella Union offered something a little more dignified, a Mexican string quartet—two harps, two guitars and a flute—and the Aguila de Oro had a black chorus.

When they entered the Varsouvienne it was getting late and Bendix put his hand on Decker's arm.

"What are we looking for?"

"I told you—"

"You must have some idea, or you wouldn't be looking."

"I'm looking for a woman with a certain cast to her eyes and eyebrows, who might look like she's gambling with her own money."

"Oh."

"Then again, she might be on a gentleman's arm, betting with his money."

"Well, Jesus, don't make it any easier."

Along the way Decker had also been having a drink or two at each bar, asking if anyone knew a woman named Julie Landan. Up until now, he had received only negative replies—or negative stares.

After the Varsouvienne Decker said, "All right, one more stop and then we'll call it a night."

"Don't tell me, let me guess," Bendix said. "The Alhambra?"

"You guessed it."

"This should be interesting."

Chapter Twenty-eight

They entered the Alhambra together, choosing at this point to abandon any pretense of not being together, and now watching each other's back.

"You want to gamble, or drink?" Bendix asked.

Decker looked around for Annie Tucker, and when he didn't see her in the casino he said, "Drink."

"How about something to eat?"

"Sure, why not?"

"Unless you think that's pushing it."

"I don't think they'll poison our food."

Bendix made a face at the unpleasant thought, and they walked to the dining room, where there were not only tables, but a small bar. Decker saw Annie Tucker standing at the bar with a man, looking bored. The man was looking at her with obvious relish.

Decker and Bendix were seated, and Bendix saw Decker look towards the bar.

"Annie Tucker a friend of yours?" Bendix asked.

"Does everyone in town know who she is?"

"Anyone who's ever been in Portsmouth Square does. When Van Gelder first hired her he squired her around on his arm, taking her to dinner at all the Portsmouth Square hotels."

"And then he turned her into a whore."

Bendix shrugged.

"Who knows what turns a woman into a whore, but I'll giver her this. She's not just a whore. That lady has a lot of class."

"To much for this place, I think."

"You may be right."

Finally, Annie Tucker's bored eyes began to wander about the room and fell on Decker. He waved her over. She said something to her companion, put her hand on his arm, and then walked over to Decker's table.

"This isn't smart, you know," she said to Decker. She looked at Bendix and said, "Mr. Bendix."

"Miss Tucker."

"Not particular about the company you keep, I see."

"Would you join us for something to eat?" Decker asked.

"Oh, sure. That's all Van Gelder would have to see."

"Don't tell me he doesn't like me?" Decker asked.

"He didn't tell me in so many words—"

"Does he know you were at the Ballard House earlier today?"

The worried look came over her face and she said, "I don't know."

"What do you think?"

"I think he knows, but I don't know why he hasn't asked me about it."

"Annie, why don't you just leave here with us and come over to the Ballard House."

"I can't."

"You don't have to work there, just stay with Sally for a while."

"I can't," she repeated more stridently than before.

"Then maybe Sally was right."

"About what?"

"She said she thought Van Gelder had something on you to keep you here."

"She said what?" Annie Tucker asked, looking surprised.

"Maybe she's a little smarter than you give her credit for."

"She may be smart, but she's wrong," she said. "Van Gelder has nothing on me."

"Then why stay?"

"It's . . . it's a job, and I couldn't get paid as much anywhere else."

"Come on," Decker said, "there are plenty of hotels in the Square who could pay you as much."

"But they won't."

"What do you mean?"

She frowned and said, "I have to go back to work before someone sees us talking."

"Annie—" he said as she turned away, but stopped short when he—and Annie—both saw Mark Sideman watching them from the doorway. She nodded to Sideman, then walked over and rejoined her companion at the bar. She looked much more animated now, probably for Sideman's benefit.

"What's going on?" Bendix asked. "That wasn't what I understood we were coming here for."

"Just doing a favor for a friend," Decker said. "You really want to eat here?"

"No. Let's go."

They got up and left, walking past Sideman, who said nothing.

On the way back to the Ballard House Bendix said, "She was right, you know."

"About what?"

"About no one else in the Square hiring her. Not when they know she belongs to Van Gelder."

"What do you mean, she belongs to him?"

"Like everything else he has, she's his property."

"That's ridiculous. Nobody owns anybody," he said, and then thinking of the war he added, "Not anymore."

"You got a lot to learn about San Francisco."

When they reached Duke's hotel they saw that there had been some excitement. There was a broken window in the front, and three men were lying in the street. On the porch, there were three other men who looked as if they had been in a fight, but certainly looked better than the three on the ground. When Clint got closer he saw that the three men on the porch were the men Duke had hired as extra security. One of them was very large and powerfully built.

Decker and Bendix skirted the three fallen men and ascended the steps to the porch.

"Hi, Johnny," one of the men said, around his fist. He was sucking on a knuckle.

"Hi, Danny," Bendix said to Danny Peoples. "A little trouble?"

"Nothing we couldn't handle."

"Glad to hear it."

Decker and Bendix entered the hotel and saw Duke in the lobby. He was bleeding from a cut lip, and his clothes were in a state of disarray—hell, they were in shreds—but Decker saw a sparkle in the older man's eyes that he hadn't seen there in a while.

"You look like shit," Decker said.

"Come into my office for a drink," Duke said, "and I'll tell you all about it."

Chapter Twenty-nine

They went into Duke's office, accepted a drink each, and then listened while he told them the story . . .

"Apparently," Duke began, "the three men came into the hotel together, and right from the start it appeared they were looking for trouble. They went to the dining room, however, and I had only placed Danny Peoples there. I was expecting any trouble to start in the casino, so I had put Sam Mitchum and Carlos Caliente in there.

"Peoples had recognized one of the three men— a man named Palmer—and knew that he hired out for strong-arm work. He called over one of my girls and told her to go and find Duke. He did not send for Murphy and Caliente, because for all he knew there were three or four men in the casino, as well.

"Anyway, Peoples kept a sharp eye on the men, who started out by complaining about the service. When they were served, they complained bitterly— and loudly—about the food. By the time Duke arrived, they were arguing with the waiter, demanding to be brought different dinners, ones that didn't taste like piss! Imagine that? Piss! That's what Van Gelder serves in his bar!

"The waiter looked over at me at that point, and I shook my head. It was obvious that no matter what we served these three men, they were prepared to complain about it.

"At that point one of the men stood up and punched the waiter in the face. I feel bad about that. I'll have to give him a raise. Anyway, the other two men upended the table, splattering several other diners with the food that had been on it. After that they immediately turned and headed for the exit. I didn't want them in the lobby, and especially not in the casino. So Danny and I rushed to block their paths.

" 'Excuse me, gentlemen,' I said, 'but you have some breakage to pay for.'

" 'You wanna see breakage?' one of them asked. 'Come on over to the casino with us—'

" 'I'm sorry,' I told them, 'but I can't let you out of this room until you settle up.'

" 'We'll settle up—' one of them said, and he turned on Peoples and struck him. While Peoples strugged with that man, the other two began to beat on me.

"I held my own for a while," Duke was quick to point out, "but eventually they drove me back into the lobby." He paused to take a drink and then continued. "At that point, we were joined by Mitch and Carlos, and then the battle really began."

It all happened so fast that Duke didn't even have

time to draw his gun. In fact, he'd been concerned about guests being injured by possible gunplay, which was why he never did draw it.

"My boys were doing okay, though," he said. "Eventually it ended up a one on one battle and we put them out into the street."

"Did you recognize any of them?" Decker asked Bendix.

"Palmer, yeah. He's done some work for Big Harry."

"That figures," Decker said, "and Harry works for Van Gelder."

"Well, they're gonna have to do a whole lot better than they did tonight if they want to impress me."

"What happened to the window?" Decker asked.

"Oh, that was Mitch, Sam Mitchum," Duke said. "You may have noticed that he is a little on the large side."

"I noticed."

"Well, he got carried away, picked one of them up and tossed him through the window."

"Gonna make him pay for it?" Bendix asked.

Duke swallowed some more whiskey and shook his head.

"I'll pay for it."

"Shit," Bendix said, "if I broke it you'd make me pay for it."

"No, I wouldn't."

"Yes, you would."

"Not if I was in this kind of mood."

"Which is?" Bendix asked.

Duke thought a moment, then came up with a word. "Elated."

"Is that what that sparkle in your eyes means?"

"I guess. Been a long time since I've been in a brawl."

"Maybe you should get out of the hotel business and come with me," Decker said.

"Naw," Duke said. "Once in a while is fine."

"Maybe you should get cleaned up," Decker said, "I mean, just in case somebody asks to see the owner?"

"Yeah, yeah," Duke said, "you're right." He poured himself another drink and said, "Just one more drink. What did you fellas come up with?"

"Nothing," Decker said, "but I'll let Johnny tell you about it. I'm going to turn in."

"Another drink, Johnny?" Decker heard Duke ask as he opened the door.

"Sure, why not?"

As Decker was closing the door he heard Duke saying, "Let me tell you how I handled those two jokers . . ."

Chapter Thirty

Decker had just taken his shirt off when there was a light knocking on the door. He went to it and opened it and found Sally Tucker in the hallway.

"I'm sorry," she said, "I know it's late, but I was hoping to catch you before you went to sleep."

"You caught me," he said. "Come on in."

She walked past him and he closed the door. When he turned he saw that she was a little nervous. He wondered if it was him, or if she would have been nervous with any man.

"What can I help you with?"

"I heard talk that you were at the Alhambra today, and that you might be going back tonight?"

"Talk, huh?"

"Around the hotel," she said, nodding. "Did you talk to Annie?"

"I did."

"And?"

"She claims that Van Gelder doesn't have a hold over her."

"She's afraid to tell the truth."

"That may well be."

"Did you talk to Van Gelder?"

"Not about that," Decker said. "I just wanted to make him a little nervous."

"What will you do, now?"

"I don't know, Sally," Decker said. "There's not a whole lot I can do if Annie won't help."

"I'll talk to her tomorrow, then."

"That's fine, but don't go to the Alhambra. Have Duke send someone over with a message. I don't want you anywhere near that place."

"Oh, okay," she said, looking puzzled. She walked to the door, then turned and said, "Decker, do you love me?"

He was taken aback by the boldness of the question.

"No, Sally, I don't. I like you very much, but I don't love you."

"Oh. I just wanted to know. Good night."

"Good night, Sally."

Sally Tucker was just too good to believe. She was obviously just what she appeared to be, a naive young woman who had walked into a new town and new situation that she simply was not prepared to handle. She also was not prepared to accept what her sister apparently "was."

What if, Decker thought, Van Gelder really didn't have anything on Annie Tucker. How would he—or even Annie herself—make Sally understand that?

He removed his boots and was about to remove

his pants when there was another knock on the door, this one a little stronger than the one from before. Sally returning with another question?

It was Stella Morrell.

"I waited until your . . . company left."

"Sally? Don't be silly. Come on in. Would you like a drink? I've got a bottle of whiskey around here somewhere."

"No, thanks. I have to get back to the game. I wanted to see if you . . . found out anything."

"All I've really done is ask around, Stella. No one has heard—or will admit to having heard—of your sister."

"Then maybe she's not here, in San Francisco."

"Maybe not."

"But she must be," Stella said. She took out a telegraph message and handed it to Decker. "I got that today. It's a reply to one I sent."

He read it. It said that last month Stella's mother got a telegram from Julie saying that she was going to San Francisco to look for Stella.

"That doesn't mean she came, though," Decker said, handing it back.

"No, but she wouldn't tell Mama she was coming if she wasn't. I'm sure of it."

"Do me a favor, Stella."

"What?"

"Find out from your mother where Julie sent the telegram from. The would at least give us a starting point."

"All right, I'll do that. I should find out tomorrow."

"Fine."

"I'll let you get some rest, now."

"Thanks."

She turned to the door, then turned back suddenly and kissed Decker on the cheek.

"I could be persuaded to stay a little longer, Decker," she said.

Her meaning was very clear, and under other circumstances Decker might have taken her up on the offer.

"Let's wait on this, Stella. I don't want anything from you until there's nothing else going on between us. Do you understand what I mean?"

She smiled, indicating that she did. She kissed him on the other cheek and left the room before he could say anything.

Chapter Thirty-one

Julie Landan had gotten pretty friendly with the bartender in her hotel. Tonight he told her that there was a man there looking for her. In her room now, she wondered about the man who had been looking for her. Was he a detective, or the law?

When she went to bed she thought briefly about her mother and sister. She had told her mother that she was coming to San Francisco to find Stella, but as yet she had made no effort to find her sister. What would happen now if she did start looking for her? Would she walk into the arms of the man who was looking for *her*?

Lying in bed staring at the ceiling, she decided that she would have to put off locating Stella. First she had to find out who this man was and what he wanted. Once that was done, if he turned out to be someone who was after her for what happened back east—or even for something she had done here in the west—she had to find out if he could be bought off. If he couldn't be bought off, then he might have to be killed.

That shouldn't be so hard, should it? After all, she'd already killed one man who had begun to make her life hard.

What was another one?

Chapter Thirty-two

"What went wrong?" Big Harry demanded.

The three battered and bruised men faced him in a back room at the Alhambra.

"They had some good boys there, Harry," Palmer complained.

"Like who?"

"Like Sam Mitchum, for one," Murphy said, "He's as big as a house. He threw me through a window."

"Is he bigger than me?" Harry asked.

"That's a good question," Seidl said.

"Never mind," Big Harry said. "Get out. Go somewhere and lick your wounds."

"Do we still get paid?"

"Yeah, you still get paid—and be where I can find you. I may need you again—though God knows why."

The three men began to file out and Palmer hung back.

"We did the best we could, Harry."

"Sure," Harry said. "You want to come with me and explain that to Van Gelder?"

"No, thanks."

"You want another job, Palmer?"

"Like this one?"

"Easier. I want you to follow Decker as long as he's in San Francisco."

"What if he spots me?"

"I don't know," Harry said. "If he spots you I guess we'll find out, won't we?"

"Yeah, I guess so. Starting when?"

"In the morning. Report back to me every evening, right here."

"Okay, Harry. You can count on me."

"Sure. I'll remember."

Palmer nodded, then trailed his two partners outside.

Mark Sideman came walking in before the door had time to close.

"What do you want?"

"Your plan didn't work, huh, Harry?"

"I don't report to you, Sideman. I report only to Van Gelder."

"Sure. Well, he's waiting for you."

"I'll be along."

"I'll tell him."

"You do that."

The two men exchanged unfriendly glances, and then Sideman left.

After Sideman left, Harry decided that he was going to have to take matters into his own hands.

His very own hands.

* * *

Sideman couldn't have been happier. Maybe now Van Gelder would let him take care of things himself.

I guess the boys you hired weren't as good as the boys Duke Ballard hired, eh, Harry?"

Sideman couldn't believe his ears. Van Gelder was going to let Harry off scott free, without an ounce of blame?

"He hired the best, Mr. Van Gelder," Harry said, "which explains why I wasn't able to find them."

"Buy them off."

"That don't happen, Mr. Van Gelder," Harry said. "You know that. That'd be like somebody trying to buy me off."

"And that doesn't happen, huh?"

"Never."

Van Gelder rubbed his jaw.

"Maybe we need outside help."

"You talking hired guns, Mr. Van Gelder?"

"I don't know if the situation calls for that, yet."

"All Ballard did was hire one of your girls," Harry pointed out.

"Sure," Sideman said. "Why was that so bad, right? He took Annie's sister, maybe he'll take Annie next."

Van Gelder shook his head.

"He can't get Annie Tucker. I've got her sewed up tight."

"That don't mean he won't try," Sideman said. "After all, he brought Decker in, didn't he?"

"Maybe we should check Decker out."

Harry was nodding when Sideman said, "I already have."

Van Gelder looked at him in surprise.

"And?"

"He's been a bounty hunter for the past five years or so, maybe more. He's got a good record. Usually gets his man when he goes after him."

"So what's he doing in San Francisco?"

"He's friends with Ballard. Maybe Ballard called him in to help."

"Help on what?"

"Maybe he's looking to move into the Square," Sideman suggested, "with the Alhambra."

"Never!"

"I didn't think—" Harry started to say.

"Good, Harry," Sideman said. "That's not your strong suit, anyway."

"Look, Sideman—"

"Shut up, both of you," Van Gelder said. "Get out. Sideman, tell Annie I want to see her."

"Sure, boss."

Both Sideman and Harry left the room, and out in the hall they glared at each other.

"One of these days, Sideman," Harry said.

"Not in the near future, Harry," Sideman said, and started down the hall to Annie's room. It wouldn't pain him any to wake her up.

When Annie saw Mark Sideman standing in the hall she demanded sleepily, "What do you want?"

Sideman was busy inspecting her breasts, which were plainly visible through her nightie. She wished she'd pulled on a robe before answering the door.

"You're a beautiful woman, Annie."

"Tell me something I don't know, Mark. Did you wake me up to make a pass?"

"No," he said, smiling. "When I make my play, you'll know it."

"Sure. What is it?"

"Van Gelder wants you."

"Now?"

"Right now."

"What's he want?"

"What's any man want from you?"

"I'll be right there."

"Better come right now."

"As soon as I put something on," she said, forcefully. "Don't bother waiting."

He shrugged and said, "Suit yourself."

Annie closed the door and pulled on a robe. What did Van Gelder want? *Did* he want what most men wanted from her—what he wanted from her most of the time—or was he ready to talk about her visit to the Ballard House?

She'd know in a few minutes.

"I'm going to ask you a question, Annie, and I want the truth."

"You always get the truth, Victor."

"I hope so."

"What's the question?"

"Are you thinking about leaving the Alhambra?" he asked. "About leaving me?"

"No."

"You're not thinking of working at the Ballard House?"

"Why would I want to work there?"

"Your sister is there."

"My sister is better off there, Victor, and you're better off with her there. Do you know what's she's doing there? She's waiting tables—and she likes it! Is that the kind of girl you wanted working here?"

"She's naive. She could have learned."

"She's dumb, Victor. Believe me, I know. She's my sister, after all. She never would have been the kind of girl you need here."

"You mean like you?"

"Exactly like me."

"And Margot?"

"Margot!" Annie said with distaste. "She'd like me to leave the Alhambra so she could move in on you, wouldn't she? Is she the one who mentioned this to you?"

"A little bird mentioned it," he said, "just a little bird."

Sure, she thought. A vulture named Margot.

He stood up and removed his robe.

"Well, since you're here, you might as well stay the night."

"I thought you'd never ask," she said, and removed her robe.

Julie Landan woke the next morning with a plan.

The plan depended on her finding her bartender

friend during the day, because she didn't want to wait until tonight to put it into motion.

She dressed, and left her hotel. Her intention was to go to the hotel where the bartender worked and see if she could get his home address. Then she'd pay him to do what she wanted him to do, and sit back and wait.

If this worked, she could be able to start looking for her sister Stella by tomorrow.

Chapter Thirty-three

Decker was having a late breakfast in the dining room when Duke entered. He was holding something in his hand.

"Got up late, didn't you?" Duke asked, seating himself across from Decker.

"Didn't see any reason to get up early."

"How's the shoulder?"

"Fine."

In fact, his shoulder had been hurting when he woke at six, and he'd decided to give it a few more hours' rest. It was now nearly ten thirty.

"What have you got?" Decker asked.

"This is a message for you. A man dropped it off at the front desk a few minutes ago."

"What did he look like?"

Duke shrugged.

"The desk clerk didn't notice. You know, medium height, medium build—"

"Uh-huh," Decker said, opening the sealed envelope.

"What's it say? Anything important?"

Decker handed it to Duke, who read it.

YOU WERE ASKING ABOUT JULIE LANDAN LAST NIGHT. COME TO THE BLOODY BUCKET TONIGHT AND FIND YOUR ANSWERS.

                                    A FRIEND.

"Where's The Bloody Bucket."

"On the Barbary Coast. It's a bad place, Deck." He handed the message back and asked, "Who's Julie Landan? The con woman you're looking for?"

"No such luck," Decker said. "She's Stella's sister."

"Stella's sister. What the hell would Stella's sister be doing on the Barbary Coast."

"I don't know, but I guess I've been invited to find out, haven't I?"

"Are you going to go?"

"Sure, along with our friend, Johnny Bendix."

"Why don't you let me come with you?"

"They know you there?"

"Yes."

"Then stay here, Duke. I don't want to draw any undue attention."

"But this isn't even your job," Duke said. "This is just a favor."

"I do favors every once in a while, you'll remember."

"Yeah, okay, you've done enough for me, but I've returned the favor."

"So, return it now. Let me and Johnny handle it."

"Sure, okay."

Decker noticed that Duke's lip was swollen and asked, "How did you sleep last night?"

Duke touched his lip, then grinned and said, "Like a baby."

"Ruffian," Decker said, and they both laughed.

"I've got work to do," Duke said, getting up.

"If you see Johnny send him in here, will you?"

"Sure thing."

After Duke left, Decker continued to eat his breakfast with the message sitting on the table by his right elbow.

"Love letter?"

He looked up and saw Sally standing next to him.

"Just business," he said. "Could I have more coffee, please?"

"Sure."

When she came back with it Decker saw Johnny Bendix enter the dining room, look around, and then start over to him. When he reached the table Sally was still there.

"Who's this pretty little thing?" Bendix asked.

"Johnny Bendix, meet Sally Tucker, my favorite waitress."

"And now mine. Hello, Sally."

"Hello, Mr. Bendix."

"Oh, please, call me Johnny."

"Johnny . . . would you like some coffee?"

"I'd like . . ." Bendix said, then looked at the remnants of Decker's breakfast and said, ". . . whatever Decker here had for breakfast. Okay?"

"Coming right up."

Bendix watched her walk to the kitchen, then looked at Decker.

"Nice. You did say Tucker, didn't you?"

"Yep. She's Annie Tucker's sister."

"And Duke hired her away from Van Gelder?"

"Sort of."

"I can see why Van Gelder's not pleased."

"I don't see it," Decker said. "She's only one naive little eastern girl who's not fit for much more than waiting tables. She was of no use to him."

"She's very pretty," Bendix said. "He would have found some use for her."

"Well, not now."

"Duke said you wanted to see me."

"Read that," Decker said, pushing the message over to his side of the table. Bendix read it, then pushed it back.

"Are we going?"

"If it's all right with you."

"Hell, I'm being paid to watch your back. I go where you go."

"Okay."

"This isn't the one you're looking for, is it?"

"No, this is a favor."

"For her?" he asked, inclining his head toward the kitchen.

"No, but I'm doing one for her, too."

"Which is?"

"She wants me to find out why Annie Tucker won't leave Van Gelder."

"Maybe she loves him."

"I doubt that."

"Maybe he's got something on her."

"That's what she said."

"That's usually the way he works."

"How do you know that?"

"Hell, that's how he keeps Big Harry around. He's got evidence against Harry that would put him away for murder. Everybody knows that."

"Nice guy."

"So maybe he's got something on her, too, only nobody else knows about it."

"Maybe we can ask around."

"Sure."

Sally came back with his breakfast—eggs, ham, potatoes, biscuits—and Bendix broke off to watch her set it before him.

"Thanks, Sally."

"Sure. Like me to pour your coffee?"

"Please."

She leaned over to pour a cup and Decker knew that Bendix was catching the clean scent of her.

"Thank you, Sally."

"You're welcome."

She walked away and Bendix said, "Sweet."

"And young, and naive."

"She'll learn." He attacked his breakfast and after he had swallowed the first mouthful he said, "By the way, you have company."

"I do?"

"Outside, across the street. One of Harry's—or Van Gelder's—men."

"He's having me watched?"

"Probably followed."

"That's interesting."

"Means he's afraid of you."

"I can't imagine why."

"You're a mystery to him. He wants to know why you're here."

"Why I'm actually here has nothing to do with him."

"But you've gotten yourself involved in other things, besides what you're really here for, and at least one of them involves him."

"Let him sweat, then."

"What's on the agenda for today?"

"Well, tonight's the Barbary Coast, but maybe we should go over there today, just to check it out."

"Fine—uh, after I've finished my breakfast?"

Decker nodded.

"After you've finished your breakfast."

Chapter Thirty-four

They checked out The Bloody Bucket that afternoon, careful not to lose the man who was following them.

The Barbary Coast was quite different from Portsmouth Square. It was harsher and, in a way, more honest. Decker actually felt more at home there. The streets were dirt. There were boardwalks instead of paved sidewalks, and there was more equine traffic.

"This is where I should be staying," Decker said.

"I suppose you would feel more comfortable here, not being a city boy."

"Were you born here?" Decker asked Bendix.

"I was. I travelled some, but I came back. Here it is."

They stopped in front of the saloon called The Bloody Bucket.

"Do you want to go in?"

"No," Decker said. "I don't want anyone to recognize me tonight. We'll come back when it gets dark."

"We don't know who we're looking for," Bendix said, and then added quickly, "although I don't know why that should bother me. We never have."

"We'll just have to ask when we come," Decker said.

"Yeah," Bendix said, "ask questions. That's a sure-fire way to find trouble here in the Barbary Coast."

"You can always pull out."

"No, I'll tag along. Maybe I'll get a chance to see you in action tonight."

"Jesus," Decker said, "I hope not."

Julie Landan dressed in a man's shirt and loose fitting jeans, not wanting to attract too much attention. She also wore a wide brimmed stetson that had seen better days, and pulled it down over her forehead.

When she reached The Bloody Bucket she ordered a beer and took it to a back table.

She felt that by watching the door she'd know the man when he came in. He'd probably be looking around the room for her, and then he'd probably ask the bartender for her by name. Of course, the man wouldn't know who he was talking about, but by that time she'd have him picked out and would approach him. If she was wrong, she'd try again.

She began nursing her beer, and waited.

Before leaving for The Bloody Bucket Decker decided to stop in and see Stella. She wasn't in her room, so that meant she was at the game. He knocked, and when the door was opened he asked the man if she was there, and if she could come to the door. When she came to the door she stepped out into the hall and closed it behind her.

"How's it going?"

"Class is starting to tell," she said. "Luke Short is cleaning up. Do you have something?"

He showed her the note.

"I'll come with you."

"No. The Barbary Coast is no place for you—"

"You should see some of the places I've played poker, Decker."

"I know, but let me do this, Stella. If she's there, I'll bring her here to you."

Stella looked as if she was going to argue, but finally relented.

"All right," she said.

"Go inside and play poker," Decker said. "Give them hell."

"I'll try."

Outside The Bloody Bucket, Decker stopped Bendix.

"You go in first," Decker told Bendix, "and don't stop in the doorway to look around. Just go straight to the bar."

"Why?"

"Because I don't know her and I don't know if she knows me. She might be looking for someone who looks like he's looking for someone."

"That's too confusing for me," Bendix said. "I'll just walk to the bar and let you handle the rest."

"Let's go."

Bendix entered, and Decker looked back to see if Van Gelder's man was still there. He was. He had decided not to lose the man, because what he was doing here had nothing at all to do with Van Gelder.

He waited long enough for Bendix to get set at the bar, and then walked in.

Julie Landan knew him as soon as he walked in. He stopped in the doorway and searched the room with his eyes, then walked to the bar.

She waited.

The place was about half full, Decker noticed. There was a poker game going on at one table, at another two men sat with a couple of saloon girls. At a table in the back a lone figure sat with half a mug of beer. The too big hat pulled low over the brow was a dead giveaway, but he played it out.

He went to the bar, ordered a beer and asked, "Do you know Julie Landan?"

"Never heard of her, pal, but we got plenty of girls here. One of them will even let you call her Julie."

"Never mind," Decker said. He took the beer and turned his back to the bar so he could watch the room.

Finally, the figure at the back table raised a hand and beckoned to him.

As he approached the hat was pushed up from the head and he saw the face of a very pretty woman—but what he noticed first were the eyes. The shape of the eyes, and the eyebrows.

Just like the drawings on the poster.

Decker hated coincidence more than anything in the world, but it looked as if he had walked right smack dab into the middle of one.

What was he supposed to do now?

Annie was frightened.

Quite by accident she had heard Big Harry talking to about eight men in the back room that he used as an office. She had gone back there to get something for the bartender, and the door had been ajar. Harry's voice had come rumbling out, and she couldn't help but hear.

"Does everybody understand?" he was asking. "We go in there and wreck the place. Anybody gets in your way, bust him up."

"What about women?"

"Don't touch any of the women, except for Sally Tucker. Any of you remember her?"

Annie heard a couple of men say yeah, they knew her if they saw her.

"Annie Tucker's sister, right?"

"Right," Harry said. "Looks a lot like Annie."

"What do we do with her?"

"Just bring her along. Van Gelder wants to talk to her. That's it. We leave in an hour."

Annie moved away from the door quickly, almost banging into the wall in her panic.

Van Gelder was sending Harry and his gang in

to grab Sally and destroy as much of the Ballard Hotel as possible.

They had to be warned. She had to warn Sally, even if it meant that Van Gelder would turn her over to the police.

"Julie?"

She looked at him and said, "She sent me."

He laughed.

"Are we going to play that game?" he asked. "My name's Decker. Are you Julie Landan?"

"Why do you want Julie Landan?"

"I'm trying to find her as a favor for a friend," he said.

"Who's the friend?"

"Stella Morrell."

"Stella?" the woman asked, unable to hide her surprise.

"Your sister."

"My . . . my sister. What does my sister look like?"

"Like—" Decker started to say, but then the batwing doors opened and someone stepped through. "Jesus," he said. "Like that."

Julie Landan looked up at the doors and saw Stella Morrell standing there.

"Julie?" Stella asked, unsure.

As Julie removed her hat, her auburn hair fell down around her shoulders.

"Stella!"

Well, Decker thought, as the two women embraced, that answered that question. The two women were sisters. Now what was he supposed to do about the lady on his poster.

Julie Landan was the woman in the poster, the con woman he had been hunting for the reward.

How would he tell Stella Morrell about her sister?

Chapter Thirty-five

Annie ran into the lobby of the Ballard House and demanded to see Duke.

"I'm sorry, Miss—" the clerk started, but she changed her mind.

"Never mind," she said, and headed for the dining room.

"Hey!" the clerk shouted.

Annie Tucker ran into the dining room. She saw Sally standing at a table taking an order, and grabbed her sister's arm.

"Annie! What's wrong?"

"Come on, Sally. We have to get out of here."

"Why? What's the matter—"

Duke entered from behind and approached the two women.

"What's wrong, Annie?" he asked.

"Big Harry is on his way over here with eight men. They're going to wreck your hotel and grab Sally. I can't let her stay here."

"I've got a man on watch—" Duke began, but he was interrupted when someone else came running into the dining room. The diners began to watch the scene curiously.

"Duke," Danny Peoples called out. "There's a group of men coming, with Big Harry in the lead. They look like a lynch mob."

"Shit," Duke said. "Sally, take Annie into my office."

"We've got to get out—"

"It's too late," Duke said. "Do what I say!"

"Where's Decker?" Annie asked.

"He's not here now. Go! Take the back hall so you don't have to go through the lobby."

Sally grabbed Annie's arm and pulled her from the dining room.

"Danny, where are Mitch and Carlos?"

"In the casino."

"Shit, shit. Are we gonna be able to keep them out of the lobby."

"If they're not there already," Peoples said, but then they heard a crash and the sound of men shouting.

"They're here," Duke said, reaching for his gun. "Let's go."

Decker had immediately recommended to the sisters that they bring their reunion back to the Ballard House.

"I'm staying at the Parker House," Julie said.

"Let's go back to my hotel," Stella said, and Julie agreed.

Decker waved at Bendix, who joined them, and they started back to the hotel.

When they came within sight of the hotel Bendix said, "Jesus Christ. Decker, it's on fire!"

When Duke and Peoples entered the lobby they saw Big Harry lift the desk clerk out from behind the desk as if he was a baby. Another man slammed an axe into the desk several times, reducing it to splinters. A third man stepped forward and raised a lighted torch.

"Hold it," Duke shouted, but the man dropped the torch onto the remains of the desk.

Duke hit him, and all hell broke loose.

"Stella, stay here!" Decker said.

"What's going on?" Julie demanded.

"A war," Decker said.

"Let's go," Bendix said.

"Johnny, get the guy following us, and then come ahead."

"Right."

Decker ran to the hotel, mounted the steps and met utter chaos.

He heard two shots as he entered, and then a slug hit the wall near his head. He drew his gun and fell to one knee. He picked out a Van Gelder man and fired, cathing the man in the chest.

Decker knew that Duke had Peoples, Mitchum and Caliente, so anyone he didn't recognize had to be a Van Gelder man.

And then there was Big Harry.

He saw Sam Mitchum and a man who had to be Big Harry locked in battle in the center of the lobby.

The front desk was in flames, and the window curtains caught fire. From outside it looked as if the whole first floor was ablaze.

Bendix followed Decker into the lobby. He stopped him before he could join the fray.

"We've got to get those curtains down before the walls catch fire."

"I'll cover you."

Decker holstered his gun and ran for the window. He grabbed the curtains, trying to ignore the shots he heard being fired. When he had the curtains on the floor he grabbed a chair, hoisted it through the newly repaired window, and tossed the curtains outside, where they coud burn harmlessly in the dirt.

He turned, drawing his gun. He was just in time to see Duke, crouched by the stairs, catch a bullet. He saw his friend fall to the floor. He found the man who had fired the shot and fired one of his own, hitting the man in the head.

The battle had been very one-sided until Decker and Bendix arrived. Together, they turned the tide until all of Van Gelder's men were down—except for Big Harry.

Decker ran to Duke, who was bleeding from the shoulder.

"Did we get them?" Duke asked.

"We got them all, except Big Harry, and we can take care of him right now."

Decker started to rise but Duke grabbed his arm.

"Leave him to Mitch."

"But—"

"Leave him!"

They watched, then, as the two huge men traded blows in the center of the lobby. Caliente and Peoples had gone to get buckets of water and had doused the blazing remnants of the desk.

"Jesus," Bendix said, moving alongside Decker. "We gonna let them slug it out?"

"I guess so."

"I got fifty says Big Harry wins."

"You're covered," Decker said.

"I'll take some of that, Duke said.

Bendix lost.

Chapter Thirty-six

When the door to Van Gelder's room slammed open, both he and Sideman looked up from their dinner in surprise. They had been discussing Van Gelder's investment possibilities.

"What the hell is this—" Sideman asked, turning to face the door.

Decker knocked him aside with a well aimed punch, then stepped aside so Sam Mitchum could move past him with his load.

"What's going on—" Van Gelder demanded, but he was cut off when Mitchum dropped Big Harry on Van Gelder's dinner table. The table gave way and crashed to the floor. Van Gelder leaped back to avoid being crushed.

Mitchum glared at him, a piece of skin hanging down from above his left eye, which was almost entirely closed. Van Gelder felt fear in the pit of his stomach.

"Keep him away!" Van Gelder shouted.

Decker moved forward. Behind him Bendix and

Peoples stood watch. Caliente had taken Duke to a doctor.

"I want what you have on Annie Tucker, Van Gelder," Decker said.

"What? What?"

"Whatever hold you have on Annie Tucker. I want to know what it is?"

"I don't have to—"

"Mitch!"

Mitchum moved forward, as if to grab Van Gelder, who moved away.

"No, keep him away!"

"Then tell me!"

"Murder," Van Gelder said. "I have evidence that she murdered one of her customers."

"Here in the hotel?"

"Yes."

"What do you have? Witnesses?"

"Y-yes."

"Who? Who are the witnesses?"

"Look, Decker—"

"Mitch!"

Mitchum grabbed Van Gelder and lifted him up with one hand beneath his chin.

"A little pressure, Van Gelder, and you're a dead man. Who were the witnesses?"

"N-nu-nu—" Van Gelder stammered.

"Give him some air, Mitch!"

Mitchum set Van Gelder down on his feet, but kept one hand on the man's shoulder.

"Van Gelder?"

"None, there are no witnesses," Van Gelder said. "I lied."

"What do you mean, you lied?"

"She wanted to leave, and I didn't want her to, so I—we—planted—"

"You set her up?"

Van Gelder nodded.

"I had her drugged, then killed the man and put him in her room. I told her she did it."

"And she bought it."

"Yes."

"Johnny?"

Bendix stepped forward.

"Is he telling the truth?"

Bendix studied Van Gelder and then said, "Yeah, I think so."

"Mitch?"

"Yeah."

"Danny?"

"Seems like."

Decker looked at Van Gelder, then said, "You sonofabitch!" and hit him.

Epilogue

Decker and Duke were in Duke's office.

"Sure I can't convince you to stay, Decker?"

"Not that you haven't tried, Duke, but no. It's time for me to get moving."

"You didn't get what you wanted," Duke said. "Are you going to keep looking?"

Decker took a moment before replying. He thought about Sally and Annie Tucker, who now both worked for Duke. Sally was still waiting tables. Annie had been given the option to do what she wanted, and had not yet exercised it, but she was staying with Sally while she thought it over. Somehow, Decker didn't think she'd choose waiting tables, but the dining room could always use a lovely hostess. Now that Van Gelder no longer had a hold over her—a hold he'd exerted because he had loved her as he loved his possessions and didn't want to give her up—all her decisions were her own.

Then he thought about the other set of sisters he'd brought together. Stella was a gambler and would continue to gamble and travel. Julie was a con woman. Now that she had found Stella, what would she do? Would she continue to travel and work her scams, or would she go with Stella and gamble?

Whatever happened, the lives of these four women were now in their own hands. Decker took a certain amount of satisfaction in knowing that he'd had a hand in that. Also, he'd helped oust Van Gelder as the owner of the Alhambra. It remained to be seen what kind of man Sideman would become now that he was on his own.

As far as Duke's question went . . .

. . . Decker had a private conversation with Julie about her past.

"Now that you've found your sister," he'd told her, "I think it's time you put this 'con woman' career behind you."

"Oh, you do?" she asked.

"Let's put it this way, Julie. If I ever hear of you being connected with a con again, I'll come after you, and this time I'll bring you in."

"Do you really think you could?" Julie asked.

"Count on it."

Julie had regarded him silently for a few moments, then said, "I get the feeling you're a nice man, Decker. I also get the feeling you mean what you say. Okay," she said, extending her hand, "you've got a deal."

Of course, there was the fact that she had killed two people, but letting her off was a judgement call on Decker's part. Sometimes he had to play judge and this had definitely been a crime of passion.

If she'd loved her husband—and he assumed she did—then he could understand her reaction. If he ever found the men who had raped and killed Holly, he intended to kill them . . .

"No," Decker said. "I think I'm going to forget this one, Duke, and go on to the next."

"Which is?"

"I don't know, yet," Decker said, standing up to leave, "but the next outlaw will be chosen with more care than this one was. I can guarantee you that."

The Classic Film Collection

The Searchers by Alan LeMay

Hailed as one of the greatest American films, *The Searchers*, directed by John Ford and starring John Wayne, has had a direct influence on the works of Martin Scorsese, Steven Spielberg, and many others. Its gorgeous cinematic scope and deeply nuanced characters have proven timeless. And now available for the first time in decades is the powerful novel that inspired this iconic movie. (Coming February 2009!)

Destry Rides Again by Max Brand

Made in 1939, the Golden Year of Hollywood, *Destry Rides Again* helped launch Jimmy Stewart's career and made Marlene Dietrich an American icon. Now available for the first time in decades is the novel that inspired this much-loved movie. (Coming March 2009!)

The Man from Laramie by T. T. Flynn

In its original publication, *The Man from Laramie* had more than half a million copies in print. Shortly thereafter, it became one of the most recognized of the Anthony Mann/Jimmy Stewart collaborations, known for darker films with morally complex characters. Now the novel upon which this classic movie was based is once again available—for the first time in more than fifty years. (Coming April 2009!)

The Unforgiven by Alan LeMay

In this epic American novel, which served as the basis for the classic film directed by John Huston and starring Burt Lancaster and Audrey Hepburn, a family is torn apart when an old enemy starts a vicious rumor that sets the range aflame. Don't miss the powerful novel that inspired the film the *Motion Picture Herald* calls "an absorbing and compelling drama of epic proportions." (Coming May 2009!)

Paul Bagdon

Spur Award-Nominated Author of
Deserter and *Bronc Man*

Pound Taylor had been wandering the desert for days, his saddlebags stuffed with stolen money from an army paymaster's wagon, when he came upon Gila Bend. It was a wide-open town without law of any kind, haven to gunslingers, drifters and gamblers. Pound might just be the answer to a desperate circuit judge's prayers. He'll grant Pound a complete pardon on two conditions. All Pound has to do is become the lawman in Gila Bend. . . and stay alive for a year.

OUTLAW LAWMAN

ISBN 13: 978-0-8439-6015-0

☐ **YES!**

Sign me up for the Leisure Western Book Club and send my FREE BOOKS! If I choose to stay in the club, I will pay only $14.00* each month, a savings of $9.96!

NAME: _____

ADDRESS: _____

TELEPHONE: _____

EMAIL: _____

☐ I want to pay by credit card.

☐ VISA   ☐ MasterCard   ☐ DISCOVER

ACCOUNT #: _____

EXPIRATION DATE: _____

SIGNATURE: _____

Mail this page along with $2.00 shipping and handling to:
Leisure Western Book Club
PO Box 6640
Wayne, PA 19087
Or fax (must include credit card information) to:
610-995-9274
You can also sign up online at **www.dorchesterpub.com**.
*Plus $2.00 for shipping. Offer open to residents of the U.S. and Canada only.
Canadian residents please call 1-800-481-9191 for pricing information.
If under 18, a parent or guardian must sign. Terms, prices and conditions subject to change. Subscription subject to acceptance. Dorchester Publishing reserves the right to reject any order or cancel any subscription.